THE COST OF COURAGE

A NOVEL BY
KELLY ESTES

VALORMEDIA

The Cost of Courage

by Kelly Estes

ISBN: 978-1-936214-80-8

Library of Congress Control Number: 2012936088

This book is set in large type with wide leading
for improved readability.

Author photo by Ricky Barraza.

Published by Valor Media, LLC, An Imprint of Wyatt-MacKenzie

valormedia@wyattmackenzie.com

DEDICATION

This book is dedicated to those serving—to those heroes who didn't come home—to those who did, whose lives are forever changed—and to their families, now struggling for answers....

This book is inspired by the story of brothers Donald E. Fitzmaurice, Sergeant, U.S. Army Air Corps, 95th Bomb Squadron, Gunner Engineer, a *"Doolittle Raider"* who served on the crew of the *"The Green Hornet,"* and Richard W. Fitzmaurice, 2nd Lieutenant, 8th Army Air Force, Navigator on the *"Salvo Sadie,"* and depicts their service in the aerial theaters of World War II.

Pete,

Thank you for your support and your service. I hope you enjoy my novel.

Best,

Kelly

PREFACE

War is shit! I'll admit that I was mildly horrified when my great uncle uttered these words during our first conversation about his experiences as a navigator in WWII. It definitely wasn't what I expected to hear but I eventually came to find an appreciation for his no-nonsense attitude toward such a terrible subject; I eventually realized that he was trying to teach me something.

This was how, at fifteen years old, I learned the true meaning of love. It didn't come in the form of some crazy teenage crush or in the words of a romance novel. No. For me it came in the pain of a true hero who suffered both physically and emotionally for his country and who over sixty years later still mourned the loss of his brother as if it had just happened.

This was first intended as a history project, something that I approached with only an uncharacteristic passion for the subject of WWII and an interest in preserving the history of the men who fought. Little did I know it would turn into a life-changing experience for all involved and become a story that would haunt me for most of my teenage life.

The war was a subject that my mother's family rarely discussed. Until that assignment, my uncle's death had become a memory of the past and all that remained were personal recollections of this incredible person, memories that my grandmother, his sister, kept to herself for years. When I came across a news-clipping from 1946, announcing that my great-uncle Donald had been killed in war and would be receiving the Distinguished Flying Cross for his act of heroism, I was both fascinated by his courage and also saddened by the loss of a twenty-three-year-old kid who never had a chance to live, whose memory, I would soon find out never left his brother's mind.

Since my grandmother had passed, I found myself turning to my Uncle Richard for answers to my many questions about his brother. Just the mention of Donald was enough to dredge up every ounce of pain he had experienced and needless to say, I felt terrible for asking.

However, something happened during that first conversation. I quickly realized that through pain we had a connection. Though I was significantly younger than he, I too, under very different circumstances, had experienced the loss of loved ones. Understanding of the pain that went along with such tragedy helped me to only begin to fathom his terrifying experiences in war.

I will be forever grateful to my uncle for teaching me his perspective on life and for trusting a young girl with his most painful memories. This fictional story is truly a labor of love and was inspired not only by the accounts of my uncles but also by the stories of many who served as prisoners of this campaign, some of whom are still prisoners of war in their own minds.

I am honored to be connected to such heroes and will carry with me the experiences of these wonderful men who suffered for their country until the day they died. It is my hope that I can be just as brave in my life as they were in theirs, and that I will never allow the sacrifices of such valor to be forgotten.

All my love,

Kelly

STORY

They don't feed us much. It's been almost a year since I arrived and life no longer seems worth living. The men who were once strong and fearless have now deteriorated into lifeless beings that could be brought down by one punch. It is clear that they, too, have lost all hope of being rescued and have accepted their fate as casualties of this thankless war. While I share in their pain, my reasons for giving up go far beyond a diminishing hope of rescue. My hope died the day that Luke was killed on the beach in China. If that news hadn't reached my ears, I would probably be stronger than this. Now all I can do is think. As I sit in this solitary hell on what should have been a joyful Christmas Eve back home in Nebraska, I am tortured by memories of the past while my mind recreates the final moments of my brother's life.

The walls of this cell grow closer everyday. All that surrounds me is the pungent smell of death and the endless suffering that exudes from each man held captive. Eerie silence is interrupted only by the occasional bombardment of Russian artillery moving closer to the camp with each passing day. Their presence has sparked a debate among the Kriegies as to whether or not we will be liberated in the coming weeks. While more optimistic airmen are convinced that our release is inevitable, most know the Krauts too well to believe that they will relinquish thousands of prisoners without a fight. At this point, they would have nothing to lose by simply eliminating us altogether. It was thoughts like this that settled among the camp, ensuring a permanent and uneasy feeling that lingered in the minds of everyone affected.

The days pass slowly but run together like molasses making it easy to forget what happens from one to the next. For this reason, many men fear Solitary as it ensures a quicker loss of sanity. The Krauts break the weak first. In the night, cries of agony can be heard from men being abused at the hands of a Goon. The sounds of physical torture echo in this concrete hell and all the men can do is pray that the guards won't come for them next. As battered boys are returned to their cells, the gut-wrenching sounds of torture give way to moaning pain and anguish—another technique used by the Krauts to instill fear in those listening, those whose every thought was that they might be next. Me, I didn't give a shit! The only thing that I cared about, my brother, had already been taken from me and there was nothing they could do that would hurt more than the loss of such a great man.

I spent the night drying my tears and facing

the idea of life after the war without my brother. After months of speculation it was confirmed by a rebellious airman, who also found himself in a solitary predicament, that Luke was in fact the latest casualty of an ongoing war in the Pacific. As we cried together on our respective sides of the wall, it was clear that the wars had found their connection at Stalag and that I would return a "hero" with less than I had when I arrived, making any accomplishment meaningless. To the sounds of men caroling songs of joy, I drifted to sleep to the rhythm of my own tears hitting the ground.

As my body reels from the pain of my last beating my mind drifts back to the events that brought me here ... I think of Luke.

GREENVILLE, MISSISSIPPI
March 1942

I must have walked thirty miles before I was picked up. The sweat dripping down my neck was enough to attract every mosquito buzzing nearby while pits of loose gravel penetrated the soles of my boots with each step. Though I had trained for months in Mississippi, I never could get used to the heat and humidity that was characteristic of the South. It was all worth it, though, since I would get to see Luke before he left. Just before dark, a truck heading east pulled over. I hobbled as fast as I could toward it hoping to hitch a ride and ease the burden on my callused feet. As I reached the back of the truck the driver opened his door and waited for me to approach. I must have looked tired as hell because he said in a deep, southern drawl, "You look like you could use a ride, boy." I don't remember saying anything but I must have nodded or at least gestured that I needed a break from the road. He laughed and said, "Get in here, boy. You lookin' rough!" I walked around the front of the truck and hopped into the passenger's seat, tossing my bag in the back. My face was glossy with sweat and red in the cheeks as I stared ahead while trying to catch my breath. Luckily I was in good shape or that journey would have done me in. He wasted no time in getting back on the road. After a few minutes I was rested enough to get a good look at the driver and assess our where-abouts.

"The name's Al," he said. He was a middle-aged man with a scruffy black beard and teeth so rotten that most of them had fallen out. His almond-shaped eyes were surrounded by dark circles that sat above his cheeks and dark, bushy eyebrows that were angled in such a way that made him look happy and harmless to match his personality.

"So where to, son?"

"Uhh...Eglin...Eglin Field. Florida."

"Well you in luck. I's just about to drop this load but I'll take ya there. No problem taking a detour for a man in uniform, that's the least I can do."

"Thanks. Hey, I really appreciate it."

"There some reason you headed that way on foot? I know they want you's to be tough but it pretty cruel to leave you on the side of the road and make you walk to base." He chuckled under his breath. "This military business, boy?"

"I guess you could call it that. I got a letter from my mom the other night saying that my brother was shipping out in a few days. She wanted me to see him before he left since she wouldn't be able to. I got a weekend pass ... so here I am."

"Your brother, huh? You'd think that for a good kid like you the higher-ups would help you get to him."

"Yeah ... you should tell that to my Colonel. According to him what we do with our free time isn't his business so he doesn't go out of his way to help."

"You must really love your brother then. I'm sure he'd be happy you're doing it."

"Ha ... he'd tell me I'm crazy but yeah ... he's a good brother. I don't care what it takes ... I'd risk going AWOL to see him if I didn't have a pass."

"He's lucky to have you."

"Nah ... he's saved my ass so many times. I owe him this much."

"Yep, I had a brother, too. Eddie was killed in the first world war just a month before I got there."

After that he seemed content with the silence and focused on the road. All I could think about was getting there on time and being able to stay a while before having to get back. Needless to say I was getting antsy because the more time I spent on the road meant less time with Luke. As the itch from my mosquito bites grew worse, I couldn't sit still. It became so noticeable that Al looked over and saw the redness on my neck. He nodded and reached under his seat, pulled out a bottle of whiskey and said, "This'll fix ya—best medicine I know!"

We drove all night and I woke up to the early morning lights of Eglin Army Air Force Base and the roar of B-25s taking off and landing during their early morning drills. I noticed that the B-25s were taking off sooner than usual, which immediately piqued my interest. While Al remained fascinated by the sight, I wondered what it meant for Luke. "Look at that one!" Al laughed in awe like a child at an amusement park. For me the sight of planes had become less exciting. But I could understand his fascination. I simply found it funny that he was almost thirty years my senior, yet I felt like the one who had been hardened by life. It was then that I realized that I was growing up. I wasn't as fun-loving and innocent as I used to be. Now I had become responsible and determined to survive under any circumstances and I saw everything as a test of my skills and as preparation for the war I would eventually fight. I hoped to go wherever Luke was headed. I figured that we would run into each other over there and fight the enemy side by side like when we played war as kids. It could have happened, too. We were in the same branch of the service and by the time I got there we would probably end up in the same conflict only flying in different planes—mine a B-17 and his, a B-25.

When Al stopped the truck I hopped out of the passenger's side and grabbed my bag. He cried as I closed the door and stood in front of the open window. "Thank you, Sir," I told him as I reached out to shake his hand. "I really appreciate this. I'll never forget it."

In response he saluted me and said, "You

come back safe, you hear? And you tell your brother to do the same." He was terrified for Luke and me, like he knew what we were in for. I could see the fear in his eyes and the pain that he still felt for his own brother. "Write me kid...." I nodded, and decided to salute back even though it wasn't right to salute a civilian. This guy had earned it. Plus he had served. Despite the pain that wars had caused him he went out of his way to get me to Luke, and for that he was a hero.

It was about another mile to Eglin but Al had taken me as far as he could. There were rules about civilians on base and I couldn't risk trouble for my new friend. As he drove off I watched his beat-up old truck disappear down the road, all the while thinking about Eddie and how Al must miss him.

As I approached the main gate I knew something was happening. I walked up to the guard, making sure that I had my ID ready because the uniform wasn't always enough. He was less than friendly. He stared at me for a few seconds analyzing my face and then the picture on the ID. His cold eyes and wrinkled appearance were enough to put the fear of God into anyone entering the base. But he didn't scare me. I had already come this far and wasn't going to leave without seeing Luke. "What business do you have here?"

"I'm here to see my brother before he ships out. Luke Thompson ...."

"How long you here for?"

"Just the weekend."

He finally seemed satisfied with my response and said, "Go ahead—but keep your ass out of trouble while you're here."

I had no idea how to find Luke and I didn't want to ask that scruffy bastard of a guard so I figured I'd ask the next person I ran into. I wandered the base for a while before seeing any signs of life. It took some time to get to the planes from where I was. This place was worse than Greenville. The humidity alone was miserable but the hazy smog from exhaust made it even worse. It was such a relief when I finally found a hangar filled with mechanics who were welding, tearing down, and rebuilding mangled B-25s that had been to Hell and back. I walked around for a while looking at the planes. I had never really seen a B-25 up close. I couldn't get over the size compared to the B-17. They were much smaller, but seemed easier to maneuver. As I analyzed the flight chart and records on the wall a young mechanic covered in grease asked me what I was doing and who I was looking for. I told him that I was looking for my brother, Luke.

"He a Doolittle boy?" he asked.

"Yeah," I responded.

"He's out there for training. You could probably watch him land if you want. They're due back any minute."

"Thanks ...." I rattled off as I walked toward the door. He was right. As soon as I walked outside a plane was landing, but I wasn't sure if it was Luke's or someone else's. It came in hard and fast. Once it stopped I made out the words

"Lucky Lady" on the side of its fuselage. I was so enthralled in my observation of what could have been a dangerous landing that I didn't even notice all the airmen who surrounded me watching with the same amazement. Once the plane landed safely they broke out into cheers and waited for the crew to exit the aircraft. "Good one, Bradley," they shouted jokingly. "Smooth ... ." another guy said. "I think your crew is still shaken!" The pilot fired back saying "Yeah, yeah ... let's see what you can do ...." Once I saw Luke climb out of the plane I walked over to him and shook his hand.

"Look what the cat dragged in," he said. Happy I was there, he put his arm around me and we walked over to the formation of airmen anxiously awaiting the next take off. He took me aside, pointed toward the plane, and said "watch this." I stood there waiting to see what everyone was so nervous and excited about. As the pilot pulled up to a white line that had been freshly painted on the runway, some of the airmen made the sign of the cross while others were nervously tapping their hands on their legs and heckling the crew. But as the engine revved up, the chatter gave way to silence. Suddenly, the aircraft reached full speed and shot down the runway like a bullet, and when it reached the halfway point marked by a red flag, it gained altitude at a speed faster than I'd ever seen. "God damn—how the hell did they do that?" I marveled. Once the plane was airborne, the guys cheered and joked in awe of what they had just witnessed. Luke was right beside them laughing and hollering out of relief for his buddies. I had no choice but to join in.

Since that was only the seventh plane in the rotation there were still quite a few left to go. Luke gestured for me to leave with him. As we left the runway I couldn't help but turn around and catch one final glimpse of the next plane. I couldn't believe how quickly they were taking off. I had never seen anything like it. "What the hell was that!?" I asked Luke in a fit of excitement as we walked by the hangars. "How'd he get that plane off the ground so fast?! You guys know why they're making you do that?"

Once I reached a point of calm he responded, "That's all we've been doing for the past few weeks. You should've seen it when we first started! Doolittle got so pissed each time we fucked up, that 'assholes' became our second name. It's been hell ... I don't recommend it but Doolittle tells us it'll save our lives ... wherever we're going." As Luke was talking, I sensed an uncharacteristic fear in his voice.

We stopped at the front door of the barracks. "So you don't know where they're sending you yet?"

Shaking his head he said "No ...."

He should have known that I wouldn't let him off with that answer. As we walked through the door I continued to hound him with questions. "Come on ... they had to tell you something. Hasn't anybody asked why the need to take off so soon?"

Never one to show too much emotion he just said "Of course ... we ask and Doolittle says that he'll tell us when we need to know. I don't know what's going on but you bet you're ass it's gonna be big."

As he shuffled through his footlocker and cleared out the bottom bunk for me, I sat on the edge of the bed chewing on some jerky I had in my pocket. "So ... what did you tell Mom?" I asked.

"I didn't tell her anything ... which isn't too much of a stretch because that's about as much as I know. In the letter she was complaining about Dad and the late checks from the Corps ... same old stuff. She said she wanted to come see me but we both know she can't get down here and I'm guessing that's how you found out." He tossed me a white shirt from the pile of clothes that was now scattered across the bed, "Here ... don't say I never gave you nothin'!" Though he was happy to see me he seemed more anxious than usual. It was understandable, though. Luke wasn't much for surprises and this mission seemed like it was going to blindside all of them. I couldn't believe that a mission was so secret that even the men responsible for its execution knew as little as the next guy.

I asked Luke why he volunteered for this crap and told him how proud I was of him for all that he was doing. "You're making us proud and we love you."

"I'm just doing it because it needs to be done. Those bastards bomb the shit out of Pearl and think they're gonna get away with it … I think it's pretty clear where we're going. Better than staying home. I know Mom's worried," he said.

"Yeah … she just told me to call you before you left but I figured that since Greenville's not that far from here I could come down for the weekend. See the sights, smell the fumes. Can't ever get enough of that."

Even in his mood he chuckled. I could always make him laugh, even in the worst situations. "Take the bottom bunk … I'll sleep up top. You hungry?" He asked.

"Yeah ... starving. Haven't eaten much since Greenville."

"Well let's go ... I'll take you down to the mess hall and see what we can scrounge."

As we walked, I saw mostly women—doing laundry, running paperwork from one end of the base to the other. "What's the deal with the broads?"

"Off limits ...." he said, and ended it at that. There were some women at Greenville but nothing like these girls. We ate with the fellas in the mess hall—the food that they were serving (shit on a shingle) really hit the spot after my long trip from Mississippi. Luke's buddies were a great bunch of guys and it was easy to see how close they were as a unit.

We returned to Luke's barracks but we were the only ones there, as if his crew knew we needed some time before I had to leave, as if they anticipated it would be our last opportunity to be together as brothers. Everything was quiet.

That day, it was clearer to me that Luke would be in danger and it actually occurred to me that he may not return. I think he knew the same thing. As he climbed up to the top bunk he told me, "It's a good thing you're here."

I had never seen my brother so vulnerable. For the first time the war was real, the danger was obvious, and the reality of our situation was more apparent. While these thoughts echoed in the back of my mind, I refused to allow them to ruin my last night with Luke so I did my best to lighten the mood. "Hey ... you know where we should go when all this is over?"

"Where?"

"California."

"What's in California?"

"I just heard it's great out there, you know? Race tracks, nightclubs, bars ... lots going on ... nothin' like home."

"Oh yeah?" he asked sarcastically.

"Yeah ... a total get. Remember when we were kids and we tried to go there on Dad's wagon?"

"Ha ... yeah."

"I thought Dad was gonna have a heart attack when he found us out there. Me, you, John ... luckily it was your idea or I think we all would have been dead," I said.

"Yeah ... sometimes I miss being out there, you know?" he said.

"Yeah sure ... let's see, what do I miss most—the rotten smell of pigs, the dry, dusty heat? Can't wait to get back there." Luke knew that I was no country boy. This was one of the only things we disagreed about. Luke reveled in the slow-paced farm life while I preferred the city.

"You never appreciated it. You never took advantage of the peace and quiet out there."

"I know, I know ... hey I actually found a place I hate worse than home."

"Oh yeah?"

"Indiana," I said.

Luke laughed.

"Flight school was awful out there. Made me wish I was in Greenville. It's all your fault ...

making me sign up for this shit. Having to train in every hellhole close to home. I get killed it's on you."

He laughed a little and said "Well that's not happening ... you won't let it." "Plus Mom would kill me."

"Yeah I guess you're right ... when we played war as kids I would always win."

"Yeah sure ... you were younger—if you lost you'd cry."

"Hey ... what do you think you'll do when we get back?"

Suddenly his mood changed. He grew more reflective and told me about his dreams—something he had never done before. "I don't know ... I've always wanted to get some land, own a farm, some cattle. You know, like Dad ...."

While it didn't surprise me, I thought he could do better. "Oh yeah?"

"Yeah...just be at peace."

I thought about it for a minute. "Sounds like Hell to me but you do what you want, brother."

He laughed, "Maybe you could help me."

"Ask Dad what he thinks about that one." I was useless in the country and while I didn't know what I would do when and if I came home, I knew it would be something as far away from farming and Nebraska as I could get. After a night of laughter and conversation we fell asleep, sparing only a few hours before morning. The next day I woke to find Luke nowhere in sight. Alone in the barracks I ran outside looking for anyone around without realizing that I was still in my skivvies.

Suddenly, two decorated Officers walked toward me holding paperwork and cups of coffee. One looked like a Lieutenant Colonel and the other a Lieutenant. I had no choice but to salute them and hope that they wouldn't demand my rank and serial number for being out of uniform and idle with my time. Though I didn't officially report to them I had a nagging feeling that this would get back to my superiors in Greenville. Running back toward the barracks wasn't an option so I uttered, "Morning, Sir," to the higher ranking of the two—a stocky, balding man with a thousand-watt smile but crusty in nature. He about tossed his coffee in disbelief but seemed at the same time amused by the sight.

"Morning, son. Might I ask what you're doing in your skivvies this late in the day?" Though it was only six-thirty in the morning, to these men it may as well have been noon. "Who do you report to?" he asked as the skinny Lieutenant waited impatiently for my response.

"Actually, Sir, I'm on leave from Greenville visiting my brother before he takes off for the Doolittle mission."

"Well, that's great ... that Doolittle can be a real pain in the ass you know."

"I wouldn't know, Sir. My brother doesn't tell me much."

"Who's your brother?"

"Luke Thompson."

"Well, he's a good man."

"Yes, Sir."

"Carry on. The boys went on a run about an hour ago. Should be back any minute now. You get yourself some breakfast. I hear it's eggs this morning."

"Thank you, Sir ... I'll do that," I said, saluting once again.

"Good luck, kid." Before I knew it he and the Lieutenant had walked away. Relieved that my run-in with the higher ups hadn't gone badly, I neglected to catch their names. Not that it mattered anyway.

Moments later, Luke returned, dripping in sweat. "Hey sleeping beauty ... 'bout time you got up. They must really have you in a country club in Greenville. You'd think this was home." he said.

"Just getting my rest...nothing says I have to run with you. Should be happy I didn't go ... wouldn't want to show you up," I responded.

"Yeah, yeah get dressed ... we need to be out of here by 0700. Got a lot to do today."

"And I thought this was a vacation ...."

Once I was dressed and ready to leave, I walked out of the barracks in much the same way I had earlier—with haste, searching for any signs of Luke. It was comforting to see him standing right outside the door waiting for me. I thought about mentioning my run-in with the officers but figured it would only cause him more grief. He didn't have much time for chatter anyway. Skipping the small talk, Luke asked, "What do you know about installing gas tanks?"

"Done it once or twice on a 17. Why?"

"Don't know ... just need an extra gas tank on the plane. Doolittle told all the pilots to add them so now we need to figure out a way to make it happen."

"Well, then let's go," I said, and then asked, "Not to piss on his parade, but won't that add more weight? How are you supposed to take off?"

"We all said the same thing. He wants us to 'get rid of unnecessary weight inside' to make room for the tank and once we're done we need to test them again."

"How the hell are you supposed to do that?"

"Toss what we don't need, gear and things like that."

"They let you take handguns up there with you?"

"Probably not ... don't want the enemy getting a hold of it if we have to bail."

"Yeah, same with us," I said and paused for a moment. "You gonna take one anyway?"

"You bet your ass," he said.

"Me, too," I responded. Though it was discouraged by the Air Corps out of concern that a weapon would drop from an airman's holster on his way to the ground, most men snuck a pistol into their uniform before takeoff. No one wanted to be unarmed if confronted by the enemy. Knowing that Luke was willing to break the rules in order to protect himself and his crew eased my concerns, if only a little bit.

I hadn't been helping Luke for ten minutes before the Lieutenant Colonel came into the hangar to inspect our work. He took one look at me and smirked. "Well now, it seems like you found yourself a job."

"Yes, Sir. Seems that way," I responded. The joke was lost on Luke who wasn't aware of our meeting that morning, so he was surprised to see us so chummy.

"Sir, this is my brother Jake. He's also in the Air Corps. Just joined up a few months ago. Jake, this is Lieutenant Colonel Doolittle."

I was shocked at the realization that my first meeting with one of the greatest pilots in the history of flight had been in my skivvies, but found nothing but humor in the thought of telling Luke. Lieutenant Colonel Doolittle also seemed to revel in my discomfort.

"Yes ... well let me shake your hand, kid. I always like to see men volunteering for the air war. Beats the hell out of fighting on the ground if you ask me. Damn good choice!" he said. Suddenly, he walked over to the plane and closely examined our work. Luke and I smirked at each other awaiting his next move. Luke didn't seem surprised by his antics. We watched as he inspected every nook and cranny, dusting the fuselage with his finger. "Looks good, men."

"Thanks, Sir." He turned to Luke and said, "Sergeant … that meeting starts in ten minutes. Might want to start heading over there."

"Yes, Sir," Luke responded.

Then he looked at me and said, "Unfortunately you'll have to sit this one out, kid … one of those top secret deals …."

"No problem, Sir. I understand. I'll just stay here and finish up."

"Can't thank you enough for helping today! You've got a good brother, Thompson."

"I know, Sir." Luke nodded and patted my back, beaming with pride. As the Lieutenant Colonel left the hangar, Luke looked at me like he knew something had happened that morning but didn't want to ask. "You sure you're okay here?" he asked. "Yeah, yeah go. I got it." I hoped that the tank would help Luke—keep him safe somehow, so I wanted to be sure to do everything right, double checking my work.

I stayed in the hangar for another hour or so. Though Luke's plane was finished about five minutes after he left, I hung around to help the other mechanics who were just as grateful for the assistance. When Luke returned from the meeting, he was unable to share with me the details of the conversation. I could tell that he was itching to say something but just couldn't. Being an airman myself, I allowed my imagination to develop all possible scenarios.

Though I would love to have stayed, my weekend leave was coming to an end and if I wanted to get back in time I would have to leave soon. It wasn't likely that I would find another Al on the way back so I knew I would need as much time as possible.

Luke walked me to the front gate. Neither of us knew what to say and each step got us closer to a goodbye that we didn't want to experience. Without thinking I reached out to shake his hand. We were men now. As tears filled my eyes I wished him the best. "So I'll tell Mom I saw you," I said.

"Yeah, tell her you saw me. I'm all right ...." he assured. We stood in silence for a moment and he stared away. I never took my eyes off of him the entire time. Finally he said, "Be safe ... do what you have to. Survive. You come home, you hear. Fight and stay strong. Don't let anything happen to you,"

"Yeah, or Mom would have your ass," I joked.

"Hey ... I mean it!" he said with a more serious and somber tone, grabbing my arm to get my full attention.

"I know ... I'll get home. I promise."

"You do the same," I said. "Love you, Brother."

I had an eerie feeling as I left Eglin. I turned back just once to wave goodbye then turned around and headed for the road, never looking back. Little did I know that we would be going to separate wars fighting two very different enemies.

The road back to Greenville was different. The weather turned from sunshine to pounding rain. I didn't get a ride until the last ten miles of the trip—a crazy old lady who wouldn't shut up. I slouched into the car seat and pretended to fall asleep just so she would stop talking. I was on foot for the last mile, walking quietly through the gate at Greenville thinking about my brother and the danger that I knew he would face, all the while remembering our goodbye and the uneasy feeling that it left me with. My buddy Joe Stiegler met me at the door of my barracks holding a cup of coffee. "Thought you went AWOL on us" he said.

"No just took a little longer to get back than I thought," I responded.

"Good to see you, shithead."

"You hear the news?" he asked as he started walking away.

I chased after him, asking, "What news?"

He looked back. "The 17s are going to England … looks like Europe for us, Jake."

"Europe, huh? How are the broads?"

"Guess we'll find out," he said. "Bomb the shit out of Gerry and have 'em in the palm of our hands."

"You get a plane yet?" I asked.

"Nah, but I heard they're waiting to assign us in Savannah. Gonna be a while before that happens," he said. Stiegler and I had been buddies since flight school in Indiana. We were both training to be navigators and once we had the skills, we would be assigned to a crew in need of our services. Stiegler was the closest thing I had to a brother now that Luke was away but it was inevitable that Stiegler and I would also be separated once we were assigned to our planes. I only hoped that I could trust my new crew as much as I trusted the guys I trained with at Greenville.

DEENETHORPE AIRFIELD, CORBY, ENGLAND
November 1943

It would be another year until we saw any combat, but the training months would be brutal and rainy and made even worse with no word from Luke. By now everyone knew about the Doolittle bombing of Tokyo. It had been in all of the papers and news reels but the whereabouts of the crews were never discussed. All anyone knew was that planes took off from the USS Hornet and successfully bombed Japan in a surprise attack. Rumors that the crews were alive and well and still being used for other secret missions circulated while others suggested that it was a suicide mission in which no one but Doolittle survived. Other reports claimed that some of the men had died in crash landings while survivors were being held prisoner by the Japs. I couldn't help but think the worst but figured that if my brother had died I would have known it somehow. No one had heard from the Doolittle boys in over a year so it was likely that they were running missions in the Pacific of which even family members could not be notified. They were an elite group. The best there was, outside of the 8th Air Force, of course. If any group was to be chosen for tough missions it would be them, and there was so much concern for keeping secrets and protecting our guys at all costs, that the likelihood of them all being alive was realistic. Until I received a letter from my mother notifying me of his death or capture, for me Luke was still alive and I refused to think otherwise until my fears were confirmed.

Once I had reached Savannah at the end of

October, I waited until I got my orders to join the crew of the Missy May, whose original navigator fell sick just before they were scheduled to leave. We had a few days in the city before taking off, so I took the time to get to know the crew over shots of whiskey and cutthroat games of craps and darts. Tim Miller, the pilot, was a tough son of a bitch. He was tall and athletic, which made his former position as quarterback of his college football team believable. Even at the bar the guys followed his lead. They were all good men and I felt safe knowing that the Missy May would be equipped with such a competent squad that would have my back.

The trip to England was fairly smooth and with the exception of some thick patches of fog, we sailed through the journey, stopping only in New York, Iceland, and Greenland. On occasion, Miller would allow me to fly the plane while he napped in the back. We eventually arrived at Deenethorpe Airfield near Corby and settled into our training regimen within a few days. As navigator, I had to learn the terrain as quickly as possible since we were told that the land was similar to Berlin. My days were spent studying maps and getting familiar with the crew, which proved to be a good distraction from my fear for Luke.

In early May we left the safety of England and headed for the European Theater to engage the enemy in the air. The Japs were waiting for Luke and the Krauts were waiting for me.

Berlin, Germany
21 June 1944

It was a clear day in June—one of the nicest we had experienced since our arrival in Europe. Before that day we had flown twelve successful missions in the region and had earned our reputation as killers among the men of the 8th Air Force. We were also considered some of the luckiest sons of bitches in the entire air war because no one had survived more close calls than we had. It was true, we should have been dead or captured long before completing twelve missions with the messes we had gotten into. It was dumbass luck that all of us were still alive. On the morning of the thirteenth mission I sensed unease among the crew. Johnny D, the co-pilot, sat in the corner with an uncharacteristic blank stare. Like all of us, he was concerned about unlucky thirteen. This made me nervous because superstition had no place in war. It was poison. Breaking focus was dangerous and lead to costly mistakes. We all knew it and tried to put those thoughts out of our minds. The last thing we wanted to be was distracted.

We approached our target and dropped our load with no resistance from the enemy. I almost hated to have no opposition because it usually meant that we would run into something worse on the way back. The pessimist in me never celebrated a victory until we were back at base. We all knew better than to revel prematurely. As we headed back, the Germans dropped from the sky and surrounded us. Miller yelled over the radio, "We got company, boys."

"Roger, Roger let's get the hell outta here!" I replied. The only thing I hated about navigating was the fact that I was blind to the here and now. I had to rely solely on my pilot for information in order to keep track of our whereabouts and make suggestions about what to do next. To me this was a design flaw that probably caused more problems than anyone knew, but maybe that was just my desire for control in a dangerous situation. It didn't help that we had other planes flying next to us in the same formation, straight ahead, like a pack of wolves. It wasn't that I didn't trust Miller's instincts, I just hated feeling helpless. But at the end of the day I respected the fact that he was the pilot and he had the wheel.

"Fighters high 10 o'clock," yelled Smith, our Bombardier.

"Roger, Roger ... I logged the position. Stay north Miller ... gunners you know what to do." I said calmly. I could feel the Kraut ME-109s coming closer and finally caught a glimpse of one. I focused on logging our position and charting the best plan of escape. I always thought about defense when studying the routes before take-off and had developed at least three plans of escape, but experience had taught me that nothing is ever cut and dry, especially in war, so I was ready to improvise. The B-17 wasn't an easy bird to maneuver so I had to take that into consideration while strategizing. It was utilized for one purpose—to drop bombs—which is why we relied so heavily on the P-51s for an escort since they had less bulk and were usually able to give the Germans a shellacking.

"How are the Mustangs holding up?"

"Looks like two are down ... the others are barely hanging on. Hard to tell. I think we're gonna be flying solo in a few," I said.

"We've got five MEs on our tail ... get ready to defend yourselves boys. It's nowhere we haven't been before ... just do what you have to do and we'll get this sucker home." Miller was always good at the five-second pep talk. He knew just what to say to get us riled up and exactly how to calm our nerves in a stressful situation. He wasn't lying, though. It was true we had been there before. We had a couple of close calls on previous missions so we really did know the drill, but somehow that day was different. My gut feeling, coupled with the fact that it was our thirteenth, made me a bit less confident, but I couldn't think about that. I couldn't panic. I had to focus on getting home. We started taking some serious flack. Rounds were penetrating the aircraft and shattering windows, spewing debris all over the plane. I heard the first screams from gunners who had been wounded by sharp glass tearing through their flesh, but it didn't make them stop firing on the Germans. It was difficult for them to prepare for an inevitable bailout when they were so focused on defending the aircraft. Soon after, screams were coming from all sides of the plane as men were being shot in their arms and legs by enemy fire from both land and air. Everywhere I turned, bullets were tracing through the sky determined to kill anything in their path.

Suddenly, Miller yelled into the radio,

"Engines are down! Engines are down!" We lost two of our engines and the supercharger and the plane began to descend. "Cease fire and get ready to jump," Miller shouted as he sounded the bailout alarm. As the plane spiraled out of control it became increasingly difficult to move toward the escape hatch. We were losing altitude so rapidly that I didn't think we would have time to bail. I promised myself that I would make every attempt to save my buddies but the God's honest truth was that I didn't hold much hope for any of us. Between the violent crash landing and the German troops who were firing on us from the ground, death seemed unavoidable. Luckily, we were descending at an angle which pushed us further from the enemy. I encouraged the bombardier to bail with me. We were both isolated from the rest of the crew due to our positions in the plane, so we had no way of knowing what the others were doing, and by this time radio communication was lost along with the rest of the plane's electrical system. We crawled through the slender tunnel leading to the nose wheel door, which was the plane's only exit and where all the others were gathering. On the way, I tended to the wounded as best I could—plugging wounds and preparing them for bailout. I was disoriented from the constant spinning and kept falling where I stood. I pushed the guys, one man at a time, toward the door and crawled with them to the opening, pushing them out the hatch. Our pilot and co-pilot remained seated and decided to crash land along with the plane. I tried to get them to bail with us but they refused. Miller ordered me to get as many of the guys out of the plane as I could. I reassured him that I would try my hardest. Once all of the guys were out of the plane I headed toward the door, but before I bailed I turned to him and said, "I'll see you down there." As I clung to the back of the co-pilot's seat with one hand grasping the side of the door, he stared at me with a look of sorrow and fear as he nodded in response. His eyes were cold and stern. He had already accepted his fate. He turned away from me and stared ahead.

I couldn't waste anymore time. I crawled closer to the door. The ground below scared the hell out of me. I remember seeing three different shades of color every second. All I remember was dark green, which was probably trees, hazy blue sky, and golden fields of barley. It felt like I was on the worst rollercoaster ride of my life and I couldn't wait to get off. I was concerned about where I would land but I decided that staying in the plane was not an option so I just jumped. I can't even remember opening my chute but I sailed down with ease. I passed out on the short trip to the ground and awoke on impact when I hit my head and lower back on the dry, unforgiving land. I must have laid there for two minutes trying to collect myself. I probably could have laid there all day in hysteria if it weren't for the motion sickness that eventually caught up with me. The Germans were famous for their clean forests that looked like someone had just swept the ground with a broom so there was a certain irony when I covered it in vomit because of their attacks. When I stopped throwing up, I laughed hysterically at the realization. I was surprised and greatly relieved that I was still alive. The Krauts tried but couldn't succeed in killing me. I had never felt more invincible in my entire life. Of course, later I would believe that it was just dumbass luck that I didn't die that day. Something happens to you when you feel like you escaped death. You feel like you've conquered something—but more so, you just feel fortunate not to have met a worse fate. I thanked God like I never had before and decided that this would be my favorite story to tell Luke.

I had to hand it to those B-17s. They could sure take a hit. I can guarantee that if we had been flying in anything else we probably wouldn't have had a chance of surviving. Life is funny that way. I didn't know whether to be thankful for my life or to curse His name for the torture that could be awaiting us. I guess we had it coming though. After all, we were fighting a war and after twelve successful missions the enemy was bound to fire back.

I collected my chute and stood up, making sure I still had my weapon. To my surprise, it hadn't been lost in the commotion. I started looking for the crew while scouring the forest for Kraut soldiers and unfriendly civilians. My navigational training kicked in right away and I was able to pinpoint where I had landed. Judging by the distance we had flown and the landscape, I figured that we weren't far from neutral Sweden. I just wanted to keep moving and find the crew so that we would have strength in numbers against the enemy. As I roamed that forest I couldn't help but notice the ugliness of the trees and the blackened landscape that surrounded the area. The branches were like charred toothpicks which made it difficult to find cover. The ground was littered with pine needles and tan-colored dirt that were still stuck to my uniform from the jump. As I kept walking, I eventually found healthier looking trees and a few places to hide.

After an hour or so I ran into Bill, the tail gunner, who like me had also been looking for the crew. I was happy to see him. Out of all the men on that plane, I had been closest to Bill. The crew of the Missy May was a great bunch of guys but Bill was smart and funnier than hell. We were both Irish and more than a little cocky, but as a result there was a mutual respect between us.

"You find anyone yet?" he asked.

"No ... not a one. I can't imagine they dropped that far out since we all went around the same time ... but who knows ... they could be walking in a different direction."

"Yeah ... but maybe ...." he started.

"Don't even say it!" I told him. I didn't want to hear that kind of talk because it was poison in a situation like ours. As soon as you start thinking the worst, people start to die. "I'm not gonna start looking for bodies just yet. I bet they're all alive just like us."

"Tim and Johnny went down with the plane?"

"Yep," I responded and continued walking. It was hard to keep hoping for the best. I prayed that I wouldn't find any of my friends lying dead in a field somewhere. It scared me to think that just two hours earlier these guys were alive and well, just shooting the shit. Those kinds of things were dangerous to think about. I figured that it would affect me once I had time to ponder what had happened but now was not the time. I didn't want Bill to get any ideas either so I changed the subject. "You never told me any more about that sister of yours," I joked.

He laughed and said, "There's nothing to tell. She's still dating that 4F son of a bitch you met at the bar."

"Yeah and how long's that gonna last?"

"Not long I hope ... I'll put in a good word for you when we get back."

"Okay, you do that." I always asked him about his sister, Faith. She was a beauty queen from Iowa, touring with the USO on a mission to spark her singing career. Needless to say, she was a favorite among the men in the 8th Air Force. She had come to see Bill in Savannah a few nights before we left the States and went out with the guys for our last night of fun before shipping out. I had just joined the crew of the Missy May a few days earlier so I was still getting to know the guys. I walked into the bar with my buddies after our training ended and it seemed like the party had already started. We went to Smitty's Lounge for drinks and good old Faith got up and sang. "Who's that?" I asked Bill.

"My sister."

"Oh yeah?"

"Don't get too attached—she's with that guy over there." I looked at the guy he was pointing to and immediately decided that she was too good for him. He was the same age as all of us, maybe a little older, so I wondered why he hadn't joined up like everyone else. Apparently they had been together for a few months and he had decided not to join the service because of a knee injury he acquired playing football in high school.

He started working for his old man's talent company promoting Faith. Though he promised to make her a star, she didn't seem very happy with him.

I sat with Bill and the guys for most of the night drinking and having a good time but I couldn't help but watch her flirt with the group of flyboys gathered around her. I could see right through her, though, and I was probably one of the only guys who didn't give her the time of day that night. Once the fellas left the bar, I decided to stay for another round. Faith looked like she was ready to leave. She tried to get the attention of her boyfriend but was unsuccessful in breaking him away from his conversation with the club manager. "Hey pal," I told the bar tender. "I'll have another, and what are you having, Sweetheart?" I said with a bit of arrogance. She looked shocked that I would even dare to speak to her, but also relieved that she had someone to drink to with.

"Oh ... I don't know ... how 'bout a martini?"

"Sounds great, Toots. Barkeep, a martini for my new friend!" He gave us our drinks and she decided to sit back down.

"You got a light?" she asked as she pulled a couple of Lucky Strikes from her purse.

"Yeah." Even though I wasn't much of a smoker, I still had cigarettes and a lighter. They were like currency in the service. I lit her cigarette and sat at the end of the bar waiting to see what she would do next.

"So you know Bill?" she asked. "I saw you talking with him earlier."

"Yeah, he's a nice guy ... I just transferred, though, so I'm still getting to know everyone."

"They're good guys ... just don't get too attached; you never know what's gonna happen over there," she said as she blew cigarette smoke toward the bar. I could tell something else was on her mind but I didn't want to pry. I just drank. "That's the hell of it ... you get so attached and there they are—dead," she said. For a woman she was pretty worldly. I figured that she had been more affected by the war than she let on and that she might not have been as superficial as she appeared.

"You lose someone over there, Doll?" I finally asked. She looked at me and smiled, then looked down at her drink.

"Yeah, my brother ...." she said. I immediately thought of Luke. I hadn't heard from him in a while and couldn't help but worry about what might have happened to him. I knew he was on a secret mission for Doolittle but it was unusual not to have heard anything for this long. Now I was even more interested in her situation.

"What happened?"

"He died on Guadalcanal ... from what I've heard the Marines didn't have a chance. The bullets were flying from all directions and there was nowhere to run. I actually found out about it before my mother did. I ran into a Marine in Tommy's division at one of my shows ... he told me everything. I was supposed to perform a few hours later but I couldn't do it. I was too emotional so I just told them I was sick and spent the rest of the night crying in my room." As she spoke about her brother, her face grew tense like she had just woken from a nightmare. Her demeanor drew cold and dark in spite of the powder white makeup she wore. She didn't even well up. I figured that so much time had passed she was probably all cried out.

"I'm sorry to hear that," I told her, all the while terrified for my own brother but trying my best not to upset her. We both sat in silence for a few minutes thinking about family and death. I stared down at my drink believing for those few moments that I would never see Luke again.

She noticed that I was upset and immediately returned to her bubbly self. She put her hand on my arm and said apologetically, "Oh ... I'm terribly sorry for telling you about that. Here I am trying to boost the morale around here and I go and tell a story like that. I tell you, I'm the worst person for this job ... I get too attached and everything just falls apart."

I assured her that she had done nothing wrong. "Hell you guys need someone to talk to as much as anyone else ... no one can be happy all the time. I was just thinking about my brother ...." I told her.

"Oh ... is he in the service, too?"

"Yeah ... he went on a mission for Doolittle in '42 and I ain't heard from him since ...." I took another sip of beer.

"You haven't heard anything about his status either? I know that some of those guys ended up POW but a lot of them are still flying missions in the Pacific. I wouldn't worry too much about it. In this war it seems like no news is good news ... there are so many reasons you might not have heard from him yet. When Tommy died we found out right away ... there was no question. If your parents haven't heard anything, then he's probably okay." Well for whatever reason, that actually calmed my nerves about Luke.

"So most of those Doolittle guys made it out?" I asked her.

"Yeah, as far as I know, but nobody's saying much on account of the guys who are still missing ...." Either she had gotten good at telling servicemen what they wanted to hear or she actually knew what she was talking about. I figured it was the latter since she had personally experienced loss and didn't seem like she was one to bullshit.

"Now see that—you just helped me out."

She sort of laughed and said with a hint of skepticism, "Oh yeah ... and how's that?"

"You gave me some valuable information ... I think you're better at this than you think." I could tell she liked hearing that because her mood changed instantly.

She kind of laughed and said, "Well then, you're pretty easy to please ... most guys aren't happy 'til they get a song out of me or something else. They would hate to hear about my real life because it's the truth and everyone seems to want to cover that up nowadays."

"Yeah? Well luckily I'm not one of those guys."

She laughed a little and said, "You know I'm happy I met you ... you're a good one."

"That's what I hear," I told her.

"Maybe when you get back we could ...." and before she could finish, her boyfriend interrupted our conversation. He put his arm around her, making it clear that his business there was done and that he was ready to leave. He extended his hand to me and said with an heir of conceit, "Danny McPherson. Nice to meet you." I reluctantly shook his hand and told him my name. I could tell he was a shyster. He acted like he was above the world while at the same time trying to appear supportive of the guys and the war effort. He always seemed to be working a deal with someone and was profiting nicely off the war. He would put Faith in front of crowds of battered servicemen for the good of his pocketbook, caring very little about their sacrifices, or about what performing for the USO did to remind Faith of her own dead brother. With an overconfident outgoing attitude, he was trying hard to impress and prove to Faith that I wasn't good enough for her.

"Listen, I really appreciate what you guys are doing … it's great … very admirable," he said as he adjusted his pricey cuff links. It was odd to hear that from a guy who was my age; he spoke to me like he was my father. Then looking at Faith and keeping a tight grasp around her waist he said, "I know we're doing everything we can … this is how we give, you see." I glanced at Faith who looked embarrassed and apologetic and nodded to let her know that I understood and didn't blame her for his behavior.

I finally asked him, "So what kept you out of the service?"

"Well, it's not for everyone and I've got a bad knee so I couldn't join up." To me it seemed like a half-assed excuse. Some guys would fake eligibility or beg the Army to let them in—others would commit suicide if they couldn't go—yet this guy seemed relieved. But he was right about the fact that not everyone is cut out to serve. If it weren't for his conceited attitude I may have felt bad for him. I simply had no tolerance for people like that and judging by the look on her face, Faith didn't condone his behavior either. I wanted so badly to ask her about him, but I realized that Danny would see to it that we wouldn't be talking alone for the rest of the night. He started to walk her to the door and patted me on the back.

"Thanks buddy ... you get back safe, okay?" He shook my hand and I grudgingly told him that I would do my best. I appreciated his concern and probably should have been a little nicer, but the truth is we were all a little on edge about the war. He had nothing to worry about. He would be here with Faith and I would be three thousand miles away in Hell, so I didn't care. As he pulled Faith away she turned to me and said with every ounce of sincerity, "You be safe, okay? And I'll look out for your brother."

As I snapped back from that memory, I realized that something about being alone in this forest had made me think of her. I really wished that Faith were here and I know Bill was wondering if he would ever see his sister again.

All of a sudden we heard a whimpering sound followed by an agonizing cry. We both gripped our weapons and crept closer to the noise. There was a maze of shattered trees amid branches and rocks which presented obstacles for us. I hated to walk deeper into the thicket because the possibility of escape grew tougher with each step. I feared that we would encounter a wounded Kraut along with a few of his buddies and since we had minimal ammo we wouldn't be able to fend off the enemy for long. Bill and I agreed on some places to hide if the Germans seemed near so we were pretty confident in moving forward. As we moved closer, the sounds grew more intense and I saw something moving in the brush. By this time both hands were gripped on my weapon and I was ready to pop whatever came out of the bushes. Bill was just as aware. He had his weapon drawn to back me up.

Bill was a good shot so I knew he would nail anything on the first try without hesitation.

As we moved closer the moans grew more severe and right away I noticed our flight gear through the trees. Once it registered, we realized that it was our friend Sam, a gunner on the plane. He had been badly hit by the hail of bullets that followed us down after we bailed. He could barely speak. I think we both knew that he was in pretty bad shape but without thinking about it we got down on our knees and tried to plug his wounds. Blood was seeping from everywhere and it was hard to see through the layers of clothing he was wearing. We sat him up and removed everything that covered his wounds. We got our first look at his condition and it wasn't long before he began to shiver in spite of the eighty-degree weather. That was our first sign that things weren't going to end well. We tried our best to assess his condition but neither of us was a medic, so we felt pretty helpless and clumsy in our abilities. Bill was horrified by the scene and sat frozen with fear. I grabbed his face with my blood soaked hand and said "Hey ... hey ... you got morphine?" I figured he would because he usually had everything on him even if it wasn't standard issue.

"Yeah," he said, still shaken. He barely took his eyes off Sam. I told him to plug the wound in Sam's stomach with his finger until I could find a way to stop the bleeding. Sam started screaming from the pain and all I could think of was the noise drawing attention from the Krauts. Though I hated to do it, I was ready to knock him out cold with my own fist in order to quiet the area and remove suspicion. It would be a lot easier to help him that way. But eventually, Sam passed out from the blood loss, a welcome relief in what was already a stressful situation. He was in and out of consciousness for a few minutes. From what we could see, we determined that he had been shot in the neck, abdomen, and leg. I was so afraid of doing the wrong thing. I didn't know what to take care of first. I tried to remember where the arteries were and how to plug wounds but everything was happening so fast that I didn't have time to think. His pulse grew weaker and I knew he didn't have long. Bill was still in shock but intensely trying to stop the bleeding. Sam woke and stared in horror at the sight. His light blue eyes filled with tears and he tried to speak but the words couldn't come out. I held him close to me trying to keep him upright so that he wouldn't choke on his own blood. It was a horrific sight. Finally I told Bill, "Give him the morphine."

"How much?" he asked.

"All of it!" I said.

"Are you sure?" I just nodded and looked over at Sam. We both knew it would kill him but we figured it would be best. It was better than watching him suffer and bleed to death. But the morphine barely had time to work since he died minutes later. He stared up at me and closed his eyes.

Bill and I sat there in shock for a few minutes. We were both on the verge of tears but none would fall. I think we were too scared to cry. Fear will do that to you. For the first time war was real. This was no bullshit training mission. Sam wasn't coming home and we felt like we would be meeting the same fate very soon. We both took it pretty hard but we knew we had to keep moving. I was relieved that Bill was there because if I had been alone I probably wouldn't have moved. Before we could leave we had to bury Sam somewhere the Germans wouldn't find him. We hated to think that the Krauts would get a hold of him and take everything he had. We didn't have the time or the resources to bury him properly but we figured we could hide him in the thicker patches of brush that lay ahead and vowed to notify the Air Force of his whereabouts if we made it back home. We drug his body up the hill and stripped it of everything valuable. We agreed to send his belongings back to his family when we returned to England.

I grabbed one of Sam's dog tags and put it in my pocket. As I walked away, Bill stood staring at Sam's lifeless body.

"Let's go." He looked back at Sam. "You okay?" I asked.

"Yeah ... I'm fine."

"You sure?"

"Yeah ...." he said as though he were trying harder to convince himself. He looked back at Sam one last time and continued walking. We didn't speak another word about it for the next few hours. The forest went on forever.

We stopped about five miles out from where we left Sam. We were dead tired and in desperate need of food and water. Between the two of us we had a couple pieces of jerky and half a canteen of water that survived the bailout. I knelt down and studied the map still looking for a way out of the woods.

"What do you think they'll do with him?" Bill muttered.

I looked up and stared into his distant eyes and said, "I don't know ...."

I was concerned that Sam had become such an issue with Bill and worried that it was going to break him so badly that he would put both of us in danger, but a part of me knew that telling him to snap out of it would only make the situation worse than it already was. "What's going on, Bill?"

"I don't know ... just didn't expect to see that, you know. When I saw Sam laying there I didn't know what to do ... we been friends since training and ...."

To be honest I didn't know what to say. What can you say when something like that happens? It was something that he would have to deal with on his own. I was never really into religion so I wasn't about to reassure him with the canned line that everyone ends up in a better place. How should I know? At this point I had killed so many Krauts and civilians I wasn't sure how a guy like me could end up in a better place, and since Sam was right there with me during the fire fights and bombing raids I couldn't be too sure about his fate either. Now if there is a heaven I know Luke would get in. Nothing could erase all of the good he had done during his life. With some people you just know.

I put my hand on Bill's shoulder and waited for him to collect himself. "Shit happens ... you know? Maybe he's the lucky one. I mean look at what we're going through."

He started to cry but he was careful not to make too much noise. Once he was calm he finally spoke. "There was nothin' we could do, you know? I was tryin' ... I'm sorry," he sobbed. I hated to see him blame himself for something that was out of our control.

"Hey ..." I whispered, "look at me. There was nothing we could do, okay? Nothing. You saw how bad he was hit. Even a doctor couldn't have saved him. That's why we need to make it back ... so we can bring him home before the Krauts get to him. You hear me? We need to make it back for Sam. That's the best thing we can do for him now." I didn't know if I believed any of that but it seemed to calm Bill and that was all I needed.

Bill and I kept walking, hoping to reach Sweden. We trekked through Germany. What a shithole. It was probably a nice-looking place at one point but all the artillery—Allied and Enemy—that had been laid into the land since the assault began had demolished most of the terrain, burning it to a crisp. That made our journey much harder since the barren land was rigged with rocky dirt and weeds that would strangle your feet if given the chance. It took hours to hike three miles because of the care and caution that had to be observed. Not to mention it was hot that June. Summer was just around the corner and all I could think about was Nebraska. Those arid summers prepared me for this which is why I wasn't complaining half as much as I could have been.

The sun was starting to go down on our second day of this miserable hike which made finding a place to stop our first priority. The charred landscape combined with the darkness of night would provide the cover we needed to remain unseen and get some rest. During our first night we had seen some Kraut patrols roaming the woods but none suspected that we were in the area. For that reason, we slept in shifts. Some had blood hounds whose howl would eerily liven up the darkness. We were most concerned about the dogs because they could ferret us out of our hole, even in the worst terrain. I couldn't imagine surviving a terrifying bailout only to be slaughtered by a pack of ferocious dogs while Krauts stood over us with no remorse for our pain. I tried not to think about it, but I was terrified that they would find us.

We found a cluster of trees toward the edge of the forest and decided to stop. The area was already fixed with foxholes and artillery-carved craters from previous battles, which made it easier for us to hide. The large boulders and abundant thicket that had been working against us would now helped to conceal us from the enemy, allowing us to get some shut-eye. In the craters we found remnants of Red Cross medical supplies and empty cans of food that were left by previous units. But that was as good as it got. We collected as much cover as we could, knowing that we would need it to protect our hideout for the night. Just before the sun set I felt a sharp stabbing pain in my leg. "Son of a bitch!" I whispered.

"What?" Bill asked.

"I don't know … something's in my leg." I stood up and realized that I had been grazed by a bullet. "Must have happened in the plane or on the way down." I checked that the bloody wound had clotted and figured that the pain would eventually subside. Once I had calmed my nerves, I noticed the sunset for the first time in a while. The smoke from air raids had settled into complacency creating a tropical pink phenomenon when combined with the sun. The sky, filled with a thousand shades of pink and orange, was stunning to the eye. After two days of fleeing the enemy we were now confronted with something simple and peaceful, yet something created from what had just hours ago been a horrific battle site.

"Whatchya lookin' at?" Bill asked. At first I didn't respond. As he came closer he looked out on the distance to see for himself. He asked his question again. Once I noticed him standing next to me, I finally acknowledged his presence.

"What do you think's out there?" I asked.

"A buncha shit ...." he responded, and I was happy to hear that he was back to his old self.

"Enjoy today ... you might not see tomorrow."

"How's the leg?"

"It'll be fine," I said.

Once the sun was down, pitch black darkness was all you could see. We tucked away in one of the branch-covered craters and slept as best as we could for a few hours until we heard Kraut patrols moving closer. We had to move.

Around midnight, we came across the first substantial river of our journey. I remember hearing an intense flow of rushing water as we approached the bend. There was no way around it, so we had to cross. As navigator, it was my job to know the land and the region we were in and to avoid potential dangers, but there was no conceivable way around this. Like a vein it flowed through the land and posed a distinct barrier between us and the city across the way. We had no raft. I wondered how the other guys were faring. The river was wide and treacherous and looked like it could suck us down with its rapid flow. I didn't want to die like that. As we neared the edge of the river, the tangle of twigs and tree roots that surrounded the area presented a great challenge for us. Like Luke, I hated to swim. We always joked about joining the Air Corps (what had since become the Army Air Force) so that we wouldn't have to swim. Bill wouldn't see the irony or the humor, though. It was one of those moments that only my brother would've understood and we both would've been laughing our way across the water. I couldn't wait to see him when I got home. I kept hoping that we would make it to Sweden without being caught and that the war would end soon so that we could return to our normal lives. But I had to put it out of my mind and focus on the task at hand—crossing the river. In an effort to stay as dry as possible, we bundled our flight jackets and the rest of the gear we salvaged from the plane and held it over our heads. I had my weapon in hand along with other necessities we had scrounged. With one hand reinforcing the belongings on our heads and the other sifting through the rough waters of the river we began our trek to cross. My height made walking through the deep river easier than it was for Bill, who was much shorter than I was. He could barely touch the bottom with his feet. I watched him almost drown twice and nearly lost my possessions trying to save him. I clung to my flight jacket, trying hard to keep it dry since it contained every letter I had received since my war began. My mother wrote to me almost every week as did my sisters and some of the girls I used to run with back home. I didn't want my last pieces of reality to become a casualty of the harsh current. What seemed like it would be quick to cross took at least twenty minutes. We finally reached the other side of the river and pulled ourselves up using the dirt encrusted edge. The roots that once posed a danger, served as a lifeline to keep from slipping back into the river on our way out. As I held onto the roots with my left hand, I finally felt secure enough to toss my belongings onto the dry land ahead. With both hands I pulled myself up from the raging current. I sat up on my knees and quickly took inventory of my possessions, thankful that I had made it through the harrowing ordeal. When I turned around I saw that Bill had not yet made it out of the water and was drifting downstream. It took all I had to reach him and pull him out of the river. We were both soaked to the bone and as the midnight chill set in, our teeth chattered. Always an optimist, Bill muttered that it would have been worse in the winter. We let the cold air dry our clothes and were soon able to put our flight jackets back on. I held my gun in a tight grasp. It was my only sense of security. But I knew it would be no match against a company of Germans. We walked for a few more miles, through woods and trees, broken only by flatlands. We needed to get some rest so we found another well darkened forest to camp for the night. The brush made good cover. We used our field knives to cut branches off the trees and piled dirt and rocks on top of them. Feeling safe, we hid under our makeshift shelter. Though we had planned to stay awake in shifts, Bill agreeing to take the first watch, we both fell asleep within minutes of lying down. It felt so good to rest after a long day and had we not been in grave danger, the experience could have been likened to a camping trip, falling asleep under the stars. I fell asleep thinking of Luke, dreaming of California.

Hours later, I woke to the sound of footsteps drawing close to our camp. My eyes shot open as I quietly shifted my body toward the sound. Without making too much noise I slowly lifted my hand to move some of the branches out of eyeshot. I stared straight through the opening and saw nothing. The forest grew quiet. Bill was sound asleep. I stayed still for a while then gradually pulled my gun from its holster, moving it slowly toward my chest. The footsteps sounded once again. In the pitch darkness it was difficult to see, but the steps were too large to have belonged to an animal. One step drew closer, flattening a branch in the process. The snapping of twigs was undeniable and my heart was racing. As the presence drew closer I began to breathe heavily. Before we knew it, a Kraut soldier was walking over us, crushing Bill's back. "What the fuck?" he shouted. Suddenly a voice bellowed in German and began stabbing at our pile of cover with a bayonet. Luckily, the sky lit up from a mortar blast while I jumped out from under our cover and saw the face of the man I had to kill. I had no choice. I hit him with the butt of my gun, knocking him to the ground, making him drop his bayonet in the process. He grabbed my throat and threw me back toward Bill as my weapon fell from my hand. I saw him reaching for his bayonet and kicked it with my boot. I sifted my hand through the shrubs by my side and grabbed the heaviest rock I could find, then sat up and charged toward him with an intensity I had never experienced in all of my years. I drove my knee into his chest pinning him to the ground and grasped the rock tightly in my fist. I stared him in the eyes as I pounded the rock into his head and chest time after time until he finally stopped struggling. It was awful. I was covered in blood, and desperately searched for my gun until I found it. Bill was quietly moaning in pain among the pile of branches. "Bill! You okay?"

"My back hurts like hell, Jake, feels like it's full of needles."

"Oh shit," I sat him up. "Let me see ...." I grabbed his shirt and checked his back. There was a slight graze from the Kraut's bayonet and Bill was bleeding. "All right, I see it ... don't worry—it ain't shit, just a scratch," I told him.

"He dead?" Bill asked as he looked at the

Kraut lying beside us.

"Yeah ... pretty sure." I gave him my gun and said, "Here hold this. Keep it pointed at the son of a bitch just in case. I gotta fix you up." I grabbed a handkerchief from my back pocket. "You got morphine?"

"Nah, used it on Sam, remember? I don't need it. Long as my blood and guts aren't hanging out, I'm fine," he said.

"Well long as your blood and guts aren't hanging out, I'm fine, too." As I fixed him up, Bill held his finger firm on the trigger of the gun never taking his eyes off the dead German. The light from the air raids nearby still illuminated the forest, so it was easier to see. While moving from the cover would have been a good idea, I wasn't about to leave before Bill was patched up. "You still got needles and thread in your first aid kit?"

"Yeah, inside my jacket pocket." With his hands full, I had to sift through the pockets until I found what I was looking for. "You sure I need stitches, Jake?"

"Better safe than sorry ... don't need you bleeding out on me."

"Always knew you cared," he laughed.

"Not really ... Faith finds out I saved your sorry ass she'll have no choice but to marry me when we get home."

He laughed and then grew silent. Fortunately, Bill had already threaded the needles in the kit. He would do anything to distract himself before we took off for missions, otherwise his fear would get the best of him. I never gave him shit about it. I figured his quirks kept him sharp and at this moment they were saving his life, because I never would've been able to thread a needle in pitch darkness, even with the occasional light of a mortar blast.

"Sit forward and try not to scream," I said. "You ready?"

"Yeah ... just do it." Before he could flinch I pierced his skin with the needle and pulled his wound together with each stitch of thread. He clenched his fist with the bloody handkerchief in hand and drove his forearm into the ground, still holding his gun with the other, still watching the dead German. Overall he took the pain well.

"One more and it's done … you're doing good." Once I had finished, he sat back and wiped the sweat from his face on the arm of his uniform. "You all right?" I asked again.

"Yeah …." he said. Then he looked at me. "You ok?" he asked me.

"I'm fine … that Kraut still dead?"

"Yeah you killed him good."

"You got water?" I asked.

"Nah … canteen's empty"

"Mine too … I drank from the river but not enough."

"We'll be fine. I'm sure we'll hook up with the allies in a few days," he said.

"And if we don't?" I asked.

"Hey … we're gonna be all right. Isn't that what you've been telling me? Don't take it so hard. You had to do it, Jake. It was either him or us. You had to do it." Bill grabbed my uniform. "That blood his or yours?"

I checked to make sure I wasn't injured, then responded, "His."

"Ok ... that's good, at least it wasn't you."

"You did good, bud," I told him.

"You saved my ass and I'll never forget it. We'll get through this," he responded.

I distanced myself, staring at the Kraut I had killed, not responding.

"Hey! I'll tell Faith ... or better yet, come to Iowa with me when we get back and tell her yourself."

I laughed a little, all the while believing that home was a long ways away and that we could easily meet the same fate as the dead Kraut any time, any minute, any day. "Yeah we'll see ...." I said as I crawled toward the pile of shrubbery we once had used as shelter for the night, and piled it on top of the Kraut's body. Bill now had the Kraut's gun in addition to his own while I still had mine and we spent the rest of the night with our weapons drawn.

"Why don't these Krauts ever carry anything to eat? I'm hungry as hell. Sure could go for a steak right about now," I said.

"Put it out of your mind, Jake."

We sat back-to-back, facing either direction, ready to kill whatever came our way. A few hours went by in silence before I checked on Bill. "How's the back?"

"Doing fine ... God I wish the sun would rise," he said.

"Me, too."

As dawn approached, we set off again and eventually we came across an abandoned farmhouse. The land it sat on was black from air raids. The front door was open and we entered without resistance. We moved slowly through each room, checking behind each door, ready to shoot anything that moved. Keeping in mind that we were still in the countryside near Berlin, we feared the inevitable Nazi influence at the residence. We were playing a lethal game of cat and mouse and the consequences would be disastrous if we were found.

We ended our search in the kitchen where a pot of soup was left boiling on the stove. A picture of an older man and woman with three children hung on the wall of the living room nearby. While we were happy to have found some food, we wondered where the family was and why they had left in such haste. We wondered if they had seen us coming and left out of fear, or if they were maybe hiding and waiting to attack us in defense of their home. Though we considered clearing the perimeter, neither of us wanted to walk into the enemy's grasp. We figured that staying in the house and waiting for the enemy to come to us would be the best plan. The food also made our decision to stay more attractive. Since we hadn't eaten in days, we were starving. The bowls and spoons were already laid out for us so we didn't waste any time. The entire pot of soup was finished within minutes and we felt better than we had in a while.

After enjoying our first meal in three days, we tore the place apart looking for additional food, weapons and ammo, anything we could find to sustain us as we traveled. "Ain't shit here, Bill. We need to get our asses outside and look in the barn." As we ventured out through the back door the barn appeared to be close. While it was a straight unobstructed path, there was no cover between the tree line and the barn door, perfect conditions for a sniper. "Seems quiet, Bill. You see anything?"

"No, let's just take it slow and keep as low to the ground as we can. You ready, Jake?"

"Yeah, let's get over there. Hopefully, there's a truck or something in there that we can use." As we approached, we could hear the creak of the rusty hinges on the door as an eerie breeze blew through. "Bill, when I kick it you go left, I'll go right, and anything moves, shoot it."

As we entered, the smell of fresh blood filled the barn, the same distinctive smell that had been present when we were plugging Sam's wounds. I looked up and swinging from the rafters were the bodies of a man and a woman who had been stripped and gutted. Lying on the ground at their feet was an Air Force flight jacket stuck to the ground with a bloody bayonet. I wondered whose jacket it was and could only imagine what had become of him.

"Bill we need to get the hell out of here now ... the Krauts are close. We better keep moving!"

After walking five or six miles we came across a haystack. It seemed to be the best place to hide among the mostly flat region we encountered. We managed to get some sleep before we were awakened by the sound of stabbing pitchforks and barking dogs along with the shouting of German officers grabbing us by the collar. My first instinct was to fight but before I could react they were in my face. I was the first to be pulled up from the rocky ground and before I knew it I was reintroduced to the land when I was thrown face first into the dirt. Still disoriented and groggy from my nap, I hadn't quite absorbed the situation. I guess I hadn't reacted in the way they wanted and with my vision still blurry I began to fall back asleep. Out of the corner of my eye I could see Bill on the ground next to me. I turned toward him. But before I could say anything an angry German officer was screaming in my ear. That woke me up. I felt a rifle pressing harshly against my shoulder blade and a foot in the center of my back. I don't think the officer realized that we couldn't understand his German demands and grew angrier when he didn't get the desired reaction out of us. Finally, he pulled me up while keeping the rifle pressed against my back. As he tightened his grip on my flight jacket he gave an order in German to one of the other officers in his unit. This guy didn't scream in my ear like the other one. In broken English, with a thick accent, the officer approached me and asked, "Where's your plane?" It took me a minute to process the question, so he repeated himself—this time in a harsher tone.

"I don't know. Probably forty or fifty miles

away. It's too far from here."

"And where are your friends? There should be more of you ... a whole crew. Where are they?" he demanded.

"I don't know. Some of them may have escaped but most were dead after we crashed. I think it's just me and my buddy. No one else," I responded. Though I knew that wasn't true since most of us made it out of the plane alive, I didn't want the Germans to form a search party for the others. I wanted to give them a fighting chance for escape and wanted the remains of those who had already perished to be left alone.

"You were bombing Berlin, weren't you?" he asked as if he already knew the answer.

"No ... we were just admiring the landscape and ran into some bad luck," I joked. I looked over at Bill who smirked as he continued to stare ahead. Luckily, the guards weren't proficient in English and the joke was lost on them or else they probably would've killed us both. As I would soon find out, there was no room for comedy in

Germany. At least, not within earshot of the Krauts.

As they prodded us to start walking, he continued to question. As we walked, the Kraut officer held a firm grasp on my shoulder in an effort to torture me further. Each minute hurt more than the last until my shoulder finally went numb. We had walked less than a mile when we reached a rustic farmhouse which quickly transformed into the officer's make-shift interrogation center. Once we reached the front of the house, he threw me to the ground and this time hammered me in the head with the butt of his rifle. My bleeding head hit the ground hard but I did my best to pull myself up on my forearms and assess my surroundings. I noticed that Bill had been forced to witness the ordeal and was now being moved to the rear of the farmhouse. With blood seeping from the wound on my face, I kept watch over Bill's whereabouts and tried to find a way out for the both of us. I worried about his back and hoped they wouldn't break his stitches. Once Bill was out of sight I turned toward my interrogator and tried to focus on staying alive while not revealing any information. I only hoped Bill would do the same. I was left to bear the brunt of the first officer I had encountered, the one who spoke only German. He screamed at me, but I had no answers to questions that I could not understand. I finally yelled, "I DON'T KNOW! I DON'T KNOW! WHAT THE HELL ARE YOU SAYING?" But he just kept screaming.

Suddenly, I heard shots coming from the rear of the farmhouse where Bill was being interrogated and tried to assess whether he had been killed or whether it was for my benefit in an attempt to instill fear and make me talk. There were so many things going on around me that I couldn't think straight. Training taught us to reveal only name, rank, and serial number, but doing so under such stress was tough; I uttered this information over and over. Frustrated that I was not divulging our secrets, the officer beat me with his rifle and kicked me as hard as he could in my back. The pain was so intense that I couldn't move. I was convinced that I had been paralyzed because the lower half of my body was numb. The other officer who had been nothing but an observer until then joined his buddy and started punching me in the ribs and face.

They gave me a minute to recover as I lay on the ground bruised and bleeding. I think they were surprised I was still alive. The other guy spoke English and asked me once again, "Yes or no?! Did you bomb Berlin?!"

I could hardly breathe, let alone speak, but I knew that any answer would mean another beating. It would have been so easy to say, "Yes," but I knew what that would mean, and I wasn't going to give in no matter how painful the consequences. I decided then and there that if this was the way I was supposed to die then so be it. In fact the sweet tranquility of death was looking better and better right now. I'd rather die than be taken prisoner. It wasn't up to me that day, though. The English-speaking officer grabbed me by the hair and told me to answer his question. Speaking as strongly as I could while gasping for air I replied, "Fuck you." I could hear them asking each other what I had said since my words must not have been clear the first time. I was now doubled over, spitting blood like Sam. I desperately wanted to stay in the position I was in at that moment, but before I could recover, the officer again pulled me up by the hair and asked me to repeat my answer. I think he knew we were involved in the bombings and wanted revenge. By this time in the war, the Krauts were becoming aware of their weaknesses and were desperately trying to maintain their strength over the Allies. But the Allies, particularly the Air Force, had already gained crucial control of the skies and were starting to win the war. At this moment, Bill and I were paying the price for the Germans' frustrations, so we had to stay strong until we could be rescued.

With blood gushing from my head and

painful bruises covering my body, I delivered what I thought would be the fatal blow to my existence. I smiled at the officer, with blood-stained teeth, and motioned for him to come even closer. He put his ear to my mouth and I whispered once again, "Fuck you," so clearly that there would be no question. There was no doubt that he understood; in the next moment, the butt of his rifle had separated my left shoulder blade in two and rendered me unconscious.

When I finally woke, I couldn't feel much below my lower back. I remember seeing puffs of white clouds floating carelessly in the sky as the sun offered a comforting warmth in my time of need. It had parked itself in between two clouds and sent its rays down like hands to escort me to paradise. I wondered if Sam had seen the same thing just before he died.

As I sat there waiting to die, I admired the scene, thinking, of all things, that this would have been a good day to go golfing. As kids, Luke, our brother John, and I would wait for days like this because they were perfect for golf. Before we joined the Air Corps, Luke and I worked as caddies at Green Mountain Golf Course in Lincoln. Where the name Green Mountain came from on the fields of Nebraska we never knew, but the owner took a liking to us and let us play a round after all of the wealthy club members had left for the night. At times, the members would let us take a swing or two during the day. The tips weren't bad, either. I wished in that moment that we were back at Green Mountain without a care in the world, laughing and swinging clubs. But this reminiscence didn't last long and shortly the officers sat me up on my knees and put my hands behind my back.

They wanted me to be awake for this one—maybe they thought I was already dead, who knows.

As soon as I heard the lock and load of that officer's rifle I wondered what Luke would do when he found out what happened. I hated to think about the pain and sadness my death would cause, but I kept hoping that if one of us brothers had to die that it would be me, because I couldn't live without Luke and didn't even want to try.

I stared straight at the house ahead ... I closed my eyes and awaited the shot from the officer's rifle when suddenly a German hausfrau sprinted from the entryway and tackled me to the ground coming dangerously between me and the business end of a Kraut rifle. Her left hand grasped my head and hair pushing it into her stomach and drenching her apron with the blood from my face. She bravely threw her right hand up toward the officer who now seemed determined to kill us both. She screamed intensely at the officer, "Nein, nein, bitte nein." She continued to protect me like her child and did not loosen her grasp until the officer agreed to lower his weapon. For the first time I sensed fear in the officer as he reassured the woman that he was not going to kill me. As he lowered his rifle, she stood but did not take her eyes off the weapon until it was completely lowered to the ground.

He was still visibly shaken by the ordeal and followed her commands. I could tell that he was shocked by her moxie and therefore decided to spare our lives, since he could have easily shot us both if he so desired. She soon lost interest in him and turned to focus on me. She looked down at her apron and noticed that it was stained with blood. I think she thought it may have been hers and that she was somehow injured during all of the commotion. However, after considering the placement of my head in her lap and the bloody gashes on my face, she soon realized that I was the source of the blood stains. She asked me something in German as she wiped the blood off of my face and did her best to plug my wounds attempting to stop the bleeding and seal the cuts. Judging by her motherly expression, she was probably asking if I was okay. I nodded my head, still in shock. I wanted to thank her for her brave act of kindness but I was so disoriented that no words could be spoken. I didn't know how to deal with what had happened. I was so ready to die and so accepting of my fate that I was grateful, but at the same time, disappointed. This woman was truly a hero in every sense of the word—a guardian angel in a field of Hell. What just happened didn't even seem to faze her. She tended to my wounds as if it were a routine occurrence. Though she was taking her time caring for me, the officer didn't dare interrupt. She helped me to my feet as I slowly regained the strength to move. I was finally able to get a good look at her. She was quite young. Probably my age or a little younger but beautiful in her own way and it wasn't just because she had saved my life. In fact, I hated to think that her beauty was almost wasted in an attempt to save me. She was very thin with long flowing blonde hair. Her otherwise pale skin showed signs of healthy pink in the cheeks, which was only highlighted by her blue eyes. She was a gift from God that I didn't deserve. I wanted to take her back home and marry her right then and there, and I probably would have under different circumstances.

However, the German officer had different plans for us and he finally came to his senses and yanked me away from her. Though he was pulling me away, I kept my eyes on her for as long as I could, turning toward her each time the officer pushed me closer to the road. I mouthed "thank you" but didn't want to be overly vocal for her sake. Though I was sure she spoke no English, she acknowledged the words and nodded her head, smiling slightly. Her eyes squinted as the sun held its position over the house and shone brightly. She kept watch over me as I was led away.

I soon discovered that Bill had not been killed either, as he quietly emerged from the rear of the house, prodded ahead by the English-speaking guard behind him. He didn't seem as banged up as I was, but I noticed some signs of abuse. Though I hated to see him suffer, I was sure it meant that he gave the Krauts hell just the same. I wasn't sure if he had heard the commotion with the hausfrau but I was certain that this was going to be a good story to tell him and the rest of the guys once we regrouped. Bill looked visibly shaken but still able to function as an airman.

I grew concerned for the girl since I didn't know what consequences she would face for saving me—an American—and interfering with Nazi protocol. I wanted to ask the officers what they would do to her and to beg for her protection at my own peril. I figured it was the least I could do after what she had done for me. I hated to think that she would be raped or killed as a result. I tried to ease my guilt by thinking that I didn't ask her to save me, and that she did this willingly in spite of the potential risks. Perhaps she had done this before. I made up stories about her in my head to keep me occupied on the trek to an unknown destination and decided that finding her would be my first priority after the war and that we would get married and live a life of happiness, away from the violence and cruelty that we were living in now. I couldn't wait to tell

Luke about my future wife. She was prettier than any woman I had ever seen and I was convinced that we were meant to be together.

But for now I was headed for the unknown. I figured we were going to an interrogation post nearby for some additional harassment before graduating to one of the many prison camps in the region. This was pretty standard practice from what we had heard of the guys who had escaped prison only to fly again in our unit. The abuse we had taken was unusual for the Germans, since they had a reputation for being less physical in their cruelty tactics and more focused on cultivating a psychological breakdown in their captives. However, the interrogators have no control over the officer who delivers the prisoner. Since the men in the field are half crazy and trained to kill, they don't waste time getting into your head. If they wanted an answer they'd beat it out of you, but American pilots were trained to be tough sons of bitches with something to prove, so they weren't as easy to break.

All you needed to remember out there was to keep your mouth shut and to either endure pain or bravely accept death in order to protect the secrets and your buddies.

DULAG LUFT
INTERROGATION CENTER
JUNE 24, 1944

As we approached the gate at what appeared to be our destination—a prison just outside of Berlin with a sign marked DULAG—the mood of the officers changed. Suddenly their conversation stopped and their playful attitudes toward one another changed to a somber and strict demeanor. They spoke in German to the officer guarding the ironclad door that barricaded the large footprint of drab brick structures now covering acres of once gorgeous countryside. It was clear from the poorly constructed buildings that this camp was assembled with haste and that it would not be equipped with even the most basic necessities. But I wasn't expecting much— after all it was prison. I had to focus. I couldn't miss anything. My senses were heightened amidst the fear and I became aware of every glance and change in tones of voice in conversations between the officers. I would have to survive in this hell until they moved us again. The German officer that was placed in charge of me had an M1 pointed in my back, which made me feel at ease that the Germans were becoming so desperate that they had to rely on weapons from POWs or dead American soldiers instead of their own. Fear also set in once I realized that if they had no place for us, they would resort to executing everyone in the camp to ease the burden. I didn't know, but I was determined to find answers to these questions. The officer threw me into a dark cell that was cold and wet with condensation from the ceiling above. The only illumination came from natural light seeping through the ceiling and a small square cut-out in the wall behind me, sealed by three vertical iron bars. I sat in that cell for what was close to an hour. My heart alternated between an intensely fast pace that felt like I was exploding from within to a slow and steady beat that was begging for calm serenity. I quickly realized that this was a part of their strategy. It was a mind game. Not wanting to fall victim to their plan, I did everything in my power to regain control of my mind and to calm my nerves with thoughts of home and a rescue that would surely come in a matter of time. I hoped that fear was something I could control and turn on and off as needed. I was so deep in thought that I barely noticed the German officer unlocking the door to the cell. I sat still until he leaned in to pick me up off the ground. Purposely, he grabbed me by the left shoulder which reopened the bloody gash that had been left by the butt of the gun. I wanted to kill that son of a bitch for doing that; of course that would be right after I killed the other asshole who did it in the first place. I didn't show my pain, though. I stood up and walked like a man. The officer walked me into a room, never once letting go of my bloody shoulder. The idiot wound up with my blood all over his hands and uniform but maybe that's what he wanted. That way he could remind the other prisoners on his watch that they could fall victim to Gerry's wrath at any time. He sat me down at a dirt-ridden white table in a room equipped with even filthier walls and a bright light. The room was hot and stuffy. They had stripped me of my flight jacket and uniform top when I first arrived, so I had been wearing only my white blood-stained t-shirt and pants, with nothing to protect me from the elements. I heard screams coming from the next room which must have been another inter-rogation facility. It could have been Bill since they separated us upon arrival and would probably have been doing the same thing to him as they did with me. Still, having already observed their use of mind games at the farmhouse, I wasn't going to let it affect me. They were waiting to see the sweat dripping down my face and other signs of nervousness. I think they really wanted to see me cry. What I wanted was to kill every one of those bastards and to free every prisoner in that whole goddam place. Mostly, I just wanted to survive. They saw a challenge in me and I was happy to be that challenge. I swore to myself that I wouldn't scream and cry or carry on under any circumstances. I was ready. An officer came into the room carrying a light-colored folder filled with papers. He nodded to the guard that had held post standing behind me the entire time I was seated at the table. He sat down in the chair directly across from me. I looked him in the eyes and said, "You are one ugly son of a bitch—what the fuck happened to your face? Those are the ugliest god damn potholes and scars."

As he stared at me, I stared back daring him to start a fight. I was making him nervous as he fumbled through the file. Still I never took my eyes off of him. He looked at me with a sort of respect for the way I was handling myself in the situation. He continued to read the papers in the folder and then stared over the top of the file with the coldest eyes I'd ever seen and said, "You know your brother was killed."

"Fuck you, he's not even fighting you people."

"Yes, we know ... he died in China. Just another servile American, bombing innocent civilians—women and children." I reached across the table and went straight for his throat. Two guards came from behind to restrain me as one proceeded to grab me by the hair and hold my face down until I was calm. Out of the corner of my eye I could see the interrogator sitting back with his arms folded, beaming with pride and arrogance at the reaction he had invoked. Once I was calm enough to be released from the restraint, I was allowed to raise my head and look back into his eyes.

He continued with his interrogation. "I'm sure you're very proud 2nd Lieutenant Jacob Andrew Thompson, born March 13, 1923." At this point I began to question his intelligence, but was still nervous since the birth month and date he mentioned were Luke's, but the year was mine. "We know your B-17 was flying at 35,000 feet when you bombed Berlin. Just tell us what you know and it will be better for you—we might even have a doctor look at your shoulder." I remained silent, not believing a word he was saying because none of it made sense and his facts were inaccurate. Thirty-five thousand feet couldn't be true, since no B-17 could fly that high.

Everything in me wanted to challenge his intelligence but I didn't think I could take another beating. His mistaken information actually offered a glimmer of hope that if their facts were this wrong, they were probably wrong about Luke, too.

Once the officer had had enough he looked at me and abruptly said, "Well, if you don't feel like talking, then I'll let you go back to your cell to think about your dead brother's remains scattered all over China. Maybe then you'll remember something." As I stood up to leave he said, "I like you ... you're very strong. Because I like you, I'll make you a deal. If you just tell me what I want to know, I might be able to send you home. You can be with your family ... it's up to you. Think about it."

This was tempting, but I put it out of my mind as he signaled the guard and I exited the room. I wasn't about to trust a Kraut with my life and rat out my buddies for a lie. I knew that the other airmen would feel the same way.

As I walked back to my cell I thought about Luke and wondered if the Kraut was right. Though his facts were wrong, part of me feared that Luke was actually dead. "No, no, he's full of shit," I told myself. "His Intel was all wrong—it's just another bullshit lie."

I barely slept that night thinking about Luke, believing in my heart that if he were alive he would have contacted me sometime in the last two years. My brother would not go this long without finding me. Another concern was the fact that he had not been registered as a POW, otherwise my mother would have known about it and she would have at least written to me with his status. I hated to think that she was shielding me from that kind of information, knowing our relationship. It was becoming harder to justify Luke's whereabouts and I tried to avoid thinking about him altogether so as not to take focus from my own survival.

The next morning, I heard the footsteps of a guard stop in front of my cell. The turn of a key opened the rickety door and revealed light from the hallway outside. I squinted at the harshness of the sight and placed my hand over my face to shield it from the brightness. "Get up!" he demanded. I sat up slowly, aware of my injuries and the pain that I would experience if I moved too hastily. However, my slow pace frustrated the guard who pulled me up more quickly and stood me on my feet. "Walk!" he demanded as he prodded me forward. We headed down the same dimly lit hallway that I had crossed when I arrived at Dulag and stopped only when I reached the end of a long line of airmen who were standing at the door. The guard then left my side and turned to walk back toward the cells to grab another prisoner from the room next to mine.

"Hey ... what's going on?" I asked the airman in front of me. He slowly turned to respond. His face was bandaged and bloody and the bruises on his neck were black, blue, and purple from what had no doubt been a traumatic beating. At that point I was sorry for his pain but glad they hadn't just saved their beatings for me. Without realizing it, I winced at the ugliness of his wounds, likely offending him in the process.

"We're going to prison," he responded in a British accent. He was an RAF pilot whose plane had met the same fate as the Missy May. He was in no mood to talk, but still I carried on.

"I thought this *was* prison." He smiled, then turned away. The next thing I knew, I was loaded onto a train after walking yet another three or four miles to the station, and traveled like a sardine in a packed railcar with hundreds of unfortunate airmen. In hours, we arrived at a dark, gray and depressing camp whose sign at the front access was labeled STALAG LUFT III. This would be our new home—a place that I would never forget as long as I lived.

Upon arrival, we were separated into cell block units. I wound up in North Compound where I was reunited with Bill and some of the other guys I knew from our unit. This was fortunate for all of us since the odds of such a reunion were minimal. Already things were looking up. "This might not be so bad," I thought. We were able to wander around as much as we wanted to and for the most part had our freedom, with the exception of guards watching our every move from the tops of buildings, ensuring that we saw their rifles and understood that we could be killed at any time if our behavior was unruly. We were also warned against escape since the ramifications of such an act would prove costly to everyone, not just the airman involved. If the rumors were true, the guys in Luft III were notorious for their attempts to break free, which made security a priority among the guards. Guys would talk about airmen being "turned" by the Krauts into spies who, in exchange for extra food and easier treatment, would inform the guards of any plans being made, but these guys would be quickly discovered and lose trust among the men. Others would pretend to have been "turned" only to provide false information about potential plans in order to refocus German attention away from the real efforts to escape through underground tunnels. The stories kept us entertained and aware, but I had no time for it. I wasn't about to do something stupid and end up on the run once again only to be recaptured and endure even more torture. I had been there and done that. Besides, Stalag wasn't so bad. I had access to whatever I needed: books, playing cards, my buddies' chit-chat. It was really no different than before except for the fact that we were prisoners and could not leave on our own free will. But I quickly learned that if you kept your ass out of trouble and didn't make a spectacle of yourself, the guards would leave you alone.

However, it turned out that this leniency would only last as long as the Germans knew they were safe. As soon as the Allies began to advance, the Germans regained their edge and filled Stalag with guards who were tough and hardened by war. Without the guards' knowledge, our compound had eventually gained access to a radio so we could hear the BBC reports about the war. We had been hearing for months that the Russians were advancing and this served as a good explanation for why the Germans were so nervous, observing our compounds, bringing new guards into the camp.

Around Christmas, my buddy Charlie Shaw from South Compound (who had managed to escape Stalag three times since we had arrived only to be captured and returned to solitary where he spent most of his time), hatched a plan to break out of Luft III on his own. He believed that the reason he had been unsuccessful in his previous attempts was that he had traveled with a team and that he could work better alone. Owing him a favor for some extra food he snagged for our barracks, I agreed to stand in for him during early morning roll call the day he walked out of Stalag a free man. Since I resembled his build and had the same dirty blonde hair and blue eyes that he so confidently sported, we were sure that I would be able to pass the guard's inspection with ease. I was feeling good about outsmarting a Goon as he walked past me checking the name "Shaw" on his list of Kriegies then moving on to the next prisoner, until he abruptly turned around and grabbed me by my face and called for another guard to examine the situation. "Oh shit," I thought as I prepared for an inevitable stay in Solitary, hoping that such a punishment would be the only consequence for this stupid offense. I only hoped that extra food was worth it for the shit storm this would create. The guards looked at each other and then at my face and stared in disbelief. The guys next to me in line chuckled at the sight. I wondered how far I could take this in trying to convince them that I was Shaw, but the guard who clearly knew Charlie the best was not buying it.

"Who are you?" the guard asked.

"Charlie Shaw," I responded.

He looked baffled. Then he grabbed the guy next to me by the hair and asked, "Who is he?" In an effort to protect me, that guy responded Charlie Shaw.

This went on for a while as prisoner after prisoner said the same thing, but as the guards grew more frustrated, they grabbed the last man in line and a blood hound that had been living on the property who was trained to kill without remorse, and threatened to release the dog on this poor prisoner if the truth was not revealed. I knew it was time to confess. "I'm Thompson, Jake ... North Compound. Leave him alone," I said.

"Where is Shaw?" he asked.

I hesitated for a moment, not wanting to say, but the guard once again threatened to maul the prisoner if I didn't start talking. "He left," I said.

Looking angry and ready to kill, the guard said, "HE LEFT? What do you mean he left?"

"He's gone ... I don't know. He's, he's gone ... ." I said.

The guard grabbed me by the neck and pushed me forward. I turned around to look at the row of guys lined up against the wall of the compound. They grimaced, knowing where I was headed, saluting me as a sign of good luck for my impending confinement. I don't think anyone could believe that Shaw had tried to escape again. Though I was going to pay dearly for my involvement in his plan, I hoped that he would finally make it. I only wished that I had gone with him instead of participating in the way I did, but I was ready and willing to face the consequences because the extra food Shaw and South Compound had provided for us a few weeks back helped a lot. I was more upset about missing the North/South football game that we would be playing on Christmas Day. No doubt I would be locked up for the holidays and long after as punishment.

STALAG LUFT III—SOLITARY

December 24, 1944

I sat in my cell for hours. I heard rustling in the unit next to mine and banged on the wall. "Hey ... who's there?"

"Jones, Skip Jones. You?"

"Thompson, Jake"

"I heard about you ... you're one tough son of a bitch. Giving the guards hell at Dulag the way you did. What did you do this time?" he asked.

"Stood in for Shaw from South Compound," I responded.

"Holy Shit!" he laughed, "he did it again? And you're telling me you actually had a hand in it?"

I laughed, realizing that no one in their right mind would have helped Shaw. In fact, guys willingly kept their distance so as not to be associated with his antics, but there I was, sitting in solitary while Charlie was trekking through Berlin in search of salvation. "Hey, maybe this time the guy'll actually make it and find some friends to bust us all outta here," I said.

Jones laughed and said, "Then I guess they'll give you a god-damn medal ... hell of a Christmas present, Thompson."

"Where you from?" I asked.

"Montgomery, Alabama," he responded. "You?"

"Lincoln, Nebraska."

"I went there once, nice place," he said.

"Ha ... whatever you say. You and my brother would get along well," I responded.

"He a country boy?" he asked.

"To the core ... pigs, land, the whole nine

yards."

"Sounds like me. Back home in Montgomery that's all we do is farm."

"Yeah, Luke wants to be a cattle rancher or some shit when he gets back. I know he'll be great at it," I said. For a moment, I realized that this so-called prisoner could have been placed in the cell by the Germans to get information about Shaw, but the fact that I initiated the conversation made me feel a bit better about the situation. His southern accent was too perfect for him to really be a Kraut but a lot of these guys had been turned, so it was hard to tell. It didn't matter, though. I would figure it out once they came back with the info in another interrogation. I just needed someone to talk to. Anyone.

"He in the service?" Jones asked.

"Yeah ... left a couple years ago to fight with Doolittle. Ain't heard from him since. Krauts fed me a bunch of crap when I was at Dulag about him dying in China which has to be wrong since we bombed the Japs in Tokyo," I said.

"Thompson," he pondered to himself. "Wait ... Lucky Lady's gunner?" he asked. "Luke?"

"Yes, yes! That's him!" I said. He was silent. Wait ... you know him?" I asked.

"Jake—we bombed the shit out of Tokyo, and China was the only safe passage for our guys. Jake—Luke didn't make it, he's listed MIA but they're pretty sure he's dead."

"What?"

"Yeah ... I'm real sorry."

Part of me still didn't believe it, thinking the Krauts planted this guy as another mind game to punish me for what I had done, but then I remembered meeting a Skip Jones at Eglin. He was one of the guys Luke and I ate with that first night. I also asked him questions that he could only answer if he were a legitimate airman. Soon after, my worst nightmare was confirmed when he said "the 'Lucky Lady' went down on a beach in China, and it's believed that Luke was killed on impact along with another feller."

"Who?"

"Moore." I had also met Moore—bombardier on the Lucky Lady—at Eglin. The whole thing was getting worse.

It was the worst night of my life because the nightmare was all coming together and making perfect sense. Though part of me wanted to believe that there was still hope, the reality was that I hadn't heard from Luke in more than two years and by now everyone knew that most of the planes didn't make it back without crashing. But I thought at worst he was a POW. My mother hadn't told me otherwise, but maybe that was for my own benefit unless she really didn't know that he had been killed. All of these thoughts ran through my head, torturing me. If this was a game the Krauts were playing, this time it was working. They found my weakness and exploited Luke's memory for everything it was worth. As the night went on I fought the urge to break down and instead I wept uncontrollably in silence.

Every hour or so Jones would ask how I was doing, and just before sunup he said through the muffled wall, "Don't give up—Luke wouldn't want you to give up. Don't let these bastards break you. You're probably on your way out soon."

"Yeah … aren't we all." I responded. I heard his cell door open as they moved him out of Solitary and back into the camp.

"Hang in there," he said to me. I then sat in silence for a while staring at the wall, listening to renditions of Silent Night that men in Solitary were singing. The Krauts hated when men would sing. It usually led to a beating or two for the guy who started the song, but tonight the Krauts let them be. I think I was more annoyed than anyone, but my tears served as a steady beat for the songs they were caroling and my sorrow for having learned the truth made me dread ever celebrating another Christmas with my now broken family.

After that night, weeks would go by before I saw any signs of life. My food was slipped through a hole in the door and I would sit in darkness for most of the day. New Year's came and went, not that it mattered anyway. The bone-chilling cold air wreaked havoc on my health. Each day it snowed and the men in Solitary were denied blankets and warm food which led to most of us developing pneumonia and other illnesses like hypothermia. I coughed until my lungs were sore and the harsh movements along with the chill aggravated the pain in my shoulder. It was unbearable. My shoulder was frozen and numb, tender to the touch. I began tearing the strings off of my pant legs to form a noose, hoping to braid it so strongly that I could hang myself from the bars on the ceiling, but I knew that such a plan for death would be ambitious. I stopped eating and drinking for several days in a row believing that I would starve or become so dehydrated that I would drift into oblivion but this only caused me to hallucinate so badly that I would see Luke's face in the walls of my cell. One night, I threw an entire bowl of cold soup at him screaming his name, cursing him for dying and leaving me in this solitary Hell. This form of acting out only led to a beating from a Kraut officer who was frustrated with such a careless waste of food. "Shoot me! Shoot me! Just fucking shoot me!" I begged him. He left me there, coughing black and brown phlegm onto the floor of my prison cell, crying from the pain in my shoulder.

A few days later, a Kraut officer came into my cell and picked me up by my arm. "Where are you taking me?"

"Shut up—you are too sick for us to care for here."

They threw me into the back of a truck and I had no idea where we were really going. I thought this was it—they were just going to take me somewhere and kill me. It was odd that I wasn't taken to the infirmary at the camp. Maybe they did not want me seeing anyone I knew or maybe I really was too sick to care for at Stalag.

After about an hour they stopped and pulled me out of the truck, pushing me up the walkway to what appeared to be a hospital. Once I got inside I saw that it was crowded with airmen, most of whom were American or RAF. I heard many different dialects: Australian, French, Brits, but mostly American English. Most of us were unlucky members of American crews who had met the same fate. We had all given our best effort to escape but wound up in prison just the same. While many languages were spoken, one thing was understood by all—fear. This universal language radiated off each man. This place made apparent the destruction and casualties of this war—even the doctors were nervous. No matter what your nationality, they were just trying to save lives.

The wound on my shoulder had become tender to the touch and I hated to look at it. My biggest fear was that I would leave without an arm. It seemed like everyone in that place was missing a limb. I doubt they had a say in the matter. I spent most of the time there just waiting to be seen by a doctor. As I waited I did my best to prepare for whatever they would do to me. I had heard the guys talk about gorgeous nurses standing over them when they woke from a medically induced slumber after a trip to the infirmary. That was about the only thing I was looking forward to. The doctor came into the room, followed by a nurse in a white dress. I laughed because she was just about the ugliest thing I'd ever seen. As I sat there in pain, the two looked over my chart and discussed their plan. The doctor came at me with a scalpel to examine the wound and cut away dead flesh so that he could eventually stitch up the healthy tissue. The last thing I remember was being struck in the back of the head by a Kraut officer. Anything after that was lost somewhere in my mind.

I woke in a bed, dressed in a hospital gown. The pain in my shoulder had subsided, probably due to the heavy doses of morphine that were streaming through my body. It was heaven. There was no more screaming or carrying on ... no sign of blood and guts—just silence. I lay there enjoying the quiet until familiar sounds of men

playing poker amid bouts of idle chatter interrupted the tranquility of the moment. That got
my attention and motivated me to sit up. Though
my pain had subsided considerably, I didn't want
to push it. A violent cough also served as a
reminder of the pneumonia that still plagued my
lungs, straining muscles with each movement.
My back was stiff, so I figured I had been there
for a while. The stiffness made every movement
an ordeal and the fact that I was still groggy didn't
help my situation. I grunted silently as I sat up. I
was so happy to see that my arm was still intact
and, almost forgetting about my wound, I used
it to push myself up as I maneuvered my pillow
to cushion my back.

I looked around the room and noticed that
it was filled with identical beds complete with
their own set of white sheets and damaged
servicemen who were just trying to keep it
together long enough to get home. Most of the
men were sleeping and to my surprise, all still
had their arms and legs and were in good shape.

They, too, were recovering.

"It's about time you woke up," an unfamiliar voice announced from the bed next to mine.

"Huh?" I responded, still a little groggy. He laughed and waited for me to respond. "Who are you?"

"I'm Keegan, from '50 Deuce.'"

I sat staring at him for a moment until I gained the strength to shake his hand. "Thompson from the Missy May."

Two beds over, I noticed four guys playing cards. They must have been the ones making all the noise. Everything was sore as I labored to move. As I sat up and looked toward the guys, one of them said, "We thought you'd never wake up—been there for days." I finally got a look at the guy before he turned his attention back to the cards in his hand. He was a young guy with curly blonde hair and by his accent I could tell he was from the Midwest. It was comforting to know that we were in the same situation, because if I knew anything about Midwestern boys it was that we stuck together like brothers. Coming from small towns, we grew up with an understanding that you take care of your neighbor. That's how it was with all the Americans, but with our background it didn't have to be taught and considering our situation, it was necessary for survival.

"Oh yeah?" No wonder I felt as stiff as a board.

He looked up from his hand and said, "Yeah … and you really gave the doctors a shellacking before you passed out." The rest of the guys chuckled. "You're kind of a hero around here." he said.

All of a sudden, memories from my ordeal with the doctors came rushing back. I was horrified, but figured that they had had it coming, considering the fact that their own Kraut officers were responsible for the pain I was in. But the way that it was still being discussed meant that it was probably much worse than I thought. I felt bad for the doc and the nurse … not their fault—

they were trying to help me … I didn't give it too much thought, though. People could think what they wanted. I think the men were just happy that someone finally gave the Germans what they deserved. I only wish it had been the son of a bitch who broke my shoulder instead of the doctors. As the men were relishing in the excitement which took focus off of them, I wondered what the repercussions of that outburst would be.

The men were bored … just playing cards all day. They told me to take it easy and stop trying to sit up, assuring me that my time in the hospital would probably be the best experience I would have in months. But I couldn't just lie there anymore. When I finally got out of bed, Keegan looked at me and said, "You're one determined SOB. It took you all day, but you did it."

I walked up to the window and looked outside where the only disturbance to an otherwise nice day was the occasional rumbling of a medical van bringing a new round of wounded prisoners. I figured that every new wave of wounded airmen pushed us that much closer to the door and back to Stalag. But for now I was enjoying the scenery much like I did the last time I was near death in the hausfrau's field. I asked the guys, "How long was I out?"

A skinny Italian kid from the Bronx said, "Three days—today's Thursday." All of them looked at me for a response.

I looked at them in disbelief. "Guess I needed the rest," I said.

"We were takin' bets on how long you'd be out ... you woulda stayed knocked out for another day I coulda won a hundred bucks," he said.

"Sorry to disappoint," I responded.

Suddenly, the pain in my arm grew so intense that I felt like I was gonna pass out. With pain came anger. I started to remember the Kraut son of a bitch who did this to me, and I screamed bloody murder vowing revenge before losing consciousness.

When I awoke, I found myself asking the guy

in the bed next to me what had happened. He told me I threatened the doctor and threw him into the wall just before they shot me with morphine and knocked me out. "It took three Kraut orderlies to pull your ass off the doc, you went insane!"

"You're crazy—I don't remember any of the shit you are talking about—what day is it?"

"It's Saturday, you've been out this time for two days!"

As this guy spoke I tried to sit up but then discovered that the bastards had strapped my feet to the bed.

"Oh yeah, by the way, they think you're crazy or something. I think all of these Krauts are afraid of you." I wasn't sure why he wanted to talk. "Thompson, right?"

"Yeah. You?"

"Edwards." It seemed like he had been waiting for days to tell me something but was hesitant to do so. "You have a brother fighting the Japs?"

"Yeah, I found out just before they brought me here that he was killed on the Doolittle mission."

He seemed relieved to hear that I knew. "How'd you find out?"

"Skip Jones got the word to me in solitary at Stalag. You know something I don't?" I asked.

"Well, my buddy was on that mission."

"What plane was he on?" I asked, figuring I would remember the crew from my visit with Luke.

"Seven." I could tell it pained him to remember, but he wanted me to have the whole story. "The guys were supposed to take off six hours later but the Japs spotted them. Before they knew it all hell broke loose and Doolittle decided to take off right then. Orders were to take all the shit out of their planes so the fuel would stretch farther. They got rid of everything—even the guns. The gunners had to paint broomsticks black to look like machine guns and they had to leave extra gas tanks on the ship. They all knew it was

144

going to be a suicide mission at that point...."

This got to me because I knew that the extra gas tank we installed was removed. The thing that could have saved Luke's life was left on the deck of the Hornet. It all started to make sense. For weeks, I couldn't understand how the plane would have crashed with an extra gas tank on board, but this explained everything. He continued to talk and I continued to listen.

"Fortunately, all the planes took off and they were all safe in the air for a while. They got to Tokyo and took the Japs by surprise, meeting little resistance. They bombed the shit out of the place. The Japs didn't know what the hell hit 'em. Once they completed the assault, Doolittle came on the radio and told all of the crews how proud he was of their bravery and dedication. That didn't amount to a hill of beans when they were all well aware of the fact that their fuel wouldn't hold out long enough to land in safe territory as originally planned. Doolittle left it up to the pilots ... they had to decide what to do. They knew that for the next few hours they would be in enemy territory so bad that you might as well jump out of the plane without a parachute in order to avoid the torture and lingering death that the Japs would inflict. The entire region was overrun with enemy determined to defend their homeland from what they considered a sneak attack worse than Pearl Harbor. Luckily, the fuel didn't completely burn out until they were approaching China. By then they were running on fumes just looking for a place to bail or crash land. Since most of them were still flying over the sea, bailing out didn't seem like a good idea. My buddy, as I'm sure all of the guys did, prayed that the fumes would carry them to the land which seemed so close. As they prepared for the landing the men held their positions, though the gunners and bombardiers were in the worst possible position for it." This struck me hard because Luke was a gunner. "According to my buddy, the Lucky Lady crashed off the coast of China, she came down hard in the water just shy of the beach. The impact was intense and it was a wonder how anyone survived. My buddy found out later that Thompson and Moore were killed on impact."

I didn't know what to do at that moment. I wanted so badly to cry but I just lay in silence until I fell asleep. The more I knew about Luke's death, the more it haunted me and drained me of every desire to live.

Throughout the hospital that was a restless night, unlike all the others since I had been there. Something was different, something was happening, I could feel it. The looks on the faces of the Kraut doctors and nurses had changed to somber stares as if they knew something bad was coming. For the rest of the night I tossed and turned until the sun shone through the window and awakened me.

It was about 0930 when I heard the hauntingly familiar sounds of Kraut transport vehicles pulling up in front of the hospital. The usually quiet hallways became loud with the sounds of German officers barking orders in broken

English. "GET UP YOU SURVILE FILTH! TIME TO GO BACK TO THE CAMP!" The Kraut nurse who had treated my wounds handed me a blanket for the long ride back to Luft III. Witnessing her compassion, the Kraut officer in charge slapped her across the face, knocking her to the ground. She responded, shouting a few words in German at him which made him even angrier. As she lay on the ground, the officer kicked her repeatedly in the chest and stomach until she was lifeless. He shouted, "YOU SWINE!"

Remembering the hausfrau who saved my life at the farm I wasn't about to sit by and watch this happen to an innocent person who was only doing her job. As the Kraut's attention was on the nurse, I picked up a bedpan full of piss and hit the son of a bitch over the head, hoping to knock him cold. As it turns out I only dazed the fucker, and prepared for the beating of my life.

He lunged toward me, screaming vile hatred as he focused his every punch on my shoulder and back where I had been previously injured.

He stopped just short of killing me. I was beaten so badly that Krauts had to carry me to the truck. The ride back was long and each bump in the road was more torturous than the last, worsening my pain. By nightfall we reached the gates of Stalag. The trucks drove through the gates and stopped in front of the compound's most secure structure—Solitary. Still unable to get out of the truck on my own power, the Krauts drug me out and threw me on the ground, then proceeded to drag me into that cold familiar place.

As we entered, the same evil son of a bitch who beat me for throwing soup at the wall was awaiting my return. "Jacob, I see you are back. How was your stay at the hospital?"

In my usual smartass tone I replied, "Kiss my ass, Popeye."

This drew an immediate and angry response, "THROW HIM IN! You just cost yourself another week!"

So there I would sit, in the darkness and cold, seeing my breath in the air as it escaped from tender hypothermic lips that were purple from frostbite. After weeks of rehabilitation, I was returned to the place that made me sick before my stay at the hospital. I had spent weeks paying for what Shaw had done and figured that I would never escape confinement. I was growing more paranoid by the second as I felt the walls inching toward me as each day passed to welcome another. I could hear Luke's voice in the pipes as the gray cement barrier that sectioned the room served as a canvas for his face. I crawled toward it on my hands and knees afraid to get too close but once I reached the wall, I placed my palm on the cement and watched Luke disappear from sight.

STALAG LUFT III
January 29, 1945

As the sun rose, I welcomed its light. It was comforting to know that I had survived yet another miserable night of confinement. The tears had since dried while the dirt and blood that plagued my shoulder had since dried up and turned into a noticeable scab. Almost representative of the scars in my own life. I could hear footsteps pounding down the hallway as I continued to stare blindly at the wall ahead. Suddenly the solid door opened to reveal a brawny guard dressed in black from head to toe staring down at me with the most terrifying look

I had ever seen. As he entered my cell the back of his hand along with the ring on his forefinger made contact with my cheek and opened another bloody gash. While the pain was once again unbearable I no longer had the strength to cry; a steady stream of blood replaced my tears. I lay on the ground in agony, moaning, as blood formed into a puddle on the floor. "Let's go!" he said as he pulled me onto my feet. I remained silent. After weeks of confinement I had lost my will to fight and would likely have succumbed to any demand. Walking down the hall had become terrifying. It pained me to move but it also made me weary of what was coming. I wondered about men hiding behind walls ready to jump me for my belongings. I had developed an odd sense of protection over what was mine. The only thing I looked forward to was seeing my buddies after weeks of silence.

"Maybe you'll think about the consequences next time," the guard said as we approached the door of my barracks, the blood from my cheek still fresh on his fist. I decided to ignore my desire to respond since they were looking for reasons to throw me back into Solitary for another stint. I was definitely not the same kid because this time I would return to the barracks knowing the truth about Luke. It wasn't like the other instances when I had enjoyed the silence and the chats with buddies in the cells next to mine. This time, my antics has cost me greatly, and I wondered if my dwindling desire to live would hinder my ability to protect myself and my buddies.

The guard had taken me to the barracks and I knew that once he opened the door, I would see what toll all these weeks had taken on my friends. As daylight turned to darkness I was both nervous and excited to see the men who were now the only brothers I had left. When the door opened, no one stood up. Three tattered men sat playing poker in the back corner of the room while two others slept soundly in the bunk straight ahead. Six others sat staring into oblivion, nursing their injuries without regard for their surroundings; the remaining three I later learned were out roaming the grounds, reveling in the fresh air that relieved the burden of their emotional wounds and allowed them to smoke without worsening the condition of those with pneumonia. It was a very different sight than it had been just one month earlier. However, just seeing those men worked wonders for my morale. I was happy to see that all were still alive.

"We see all you do. Never forget that!" the Goon professed just before he left the barracks. I made sure the door closed behind me before I turned around to greet my buddies. Once I could be sure he had gone, I turned around, happy to be back.

The men smiled and welcomed my return with their usual good humor. "Thought we'd never see you again."

"Yeah ... thought something better came along and you forgot about us," said another.

"Nah ... what could be better than this? I see

it hasn't changed."

"Not much ... I think the cold air's making Anderson lose his luster though."

"Yeah ... yeah," Anderson responded.

"Admit it ... you're getting rusty. At least we're not playing for real money or you'd be crying my friend."

"Hey ... you're being rude. We ain't even properly welcomed Jake back home yet."

"Oh, yeah! You're gonna love this," said Anderson.

LaMont got up and rifled through a floorboard under his bunk, pulling out a handmade basket filled with Klim powdered milk cans fashioned into candleholders with wax. The guys would use the fat layer from the top of canned soup to form a mold of burnable "wax" in the bottom of the Klim cans the Red Cross provided. Just before I was thrown into Solitary, we had started making candles for the guys planning to escape from South Compound since they needed light to see while carving the tunnels. We planned to make the candles in exchange for extra food and supplies. I was glad to see that our business enterprise was still lucrative during my long stints in the hospital and in Solitary.

"Looks good, guys!" I said as I examined the circular candles in the basket. As soon as I was done, LaMont quickly returned the basket to its rightful place under the bed so that the Krauts wouldn't get wise.

"You missed a lot, bud … maybe that'll teach ya to stand in for Shaw," said LaMont.

"I heard he got caught," said Anderson.

"Doesn't he always? That son of a bitch has had more guys thrown in the Cooler because of him … the least he could do is come up with a better plan for his escape," LaMont asserted.

"The Krauts oughtta just throw away the key."

As the debate about Shaw continued, someone said, "Hey … tell Jake what you heard on BBC the other day."

"What? What did you hear?" I asked.

"Well … it seems that our Ruskie friends are

closing in a lot faster than the Krauts expected, so we might get out of here soon."

"Or killed...." said LaMont.

"Yeah ... I've been hearing the bombs. They've been getting louder every night," I said. The Cooler (an affectionate name for Solitary) was closest to the advance and I felt bad for the poor bastards who were still there.

"Hey, maybe you and Luke could...."

I debated whether or not to break the news but I couldn't hide the pain. "Luke's dead."

"What? How do you know? Did one of those Kraut bastards say it again cuz you can't believe...."

I looked at LaMont, shaking my head and trying not to break down. "No ... it's true."

"How?"

"Skip Jones from South Compound confirmed it. He was in the cell next to mine, had been on the Tokyo Raid, came here and got captured. Once I told him who I was he put it together and well ...." I did my best to look down and focus on other things but the pain was too much. Even the sickest of the men in our barracks hopped down from their bunks and came over to offer their condolences. Some even threw empty cans of food and cartons of cigarettes in a fit of rage at what the war had taken—a testament to the bond we had formed as brothers. We had gotten to know each other's families through stories each would tell and for this reason any loss was personal, especially one that was lost in combat. No one knew what to say, but I was content with the silence. We all went to bed thinking of Luke and I believe that the pain of his death was felt by every man in the room. The news made for a difficult night, each of us wondering if we would meet the same fate very soon.

Hours later, once we had finally fallen asleep, we were awakened by the sound of dogs barking and the door to the barracks being kicked in by Kraut officers. "Get up! Get moving! Take what you have."

Those of us who weren't quick enough to get on our feet were forcibly pulled from the bed. Once out of the barracks we lined up against the side of the building with all of our possessions and were instructed to march single file to the quad. News quickly spread through the camp that the Russians were about fifteen miles out and that the guards were taking us with them as they attempted to escape on foot. Ironically, our would-be liberators were causing us more problems with their pursuit of the Germans. I grabbed Bill, still the most ill of us all, and departed for the cold night convinced that none of us would last long on this trip. Some men dragged carts and food and other belongings, but it soon got too heavy to carry so they distributed and ate the fare and tossed whatever they couldn't use onto the road.

We eventually reached an abandoned church just off the path. I saw first-hand how much damage our air raids had done. What had once been a place of peace had since deteriorated into a glorified pile of rubble that barely stood of its own strength. Even churches weren't spared as a casualty of war. Much like soldiers wounded in battle, the building's statues were missing limbs and their facial features had been altered from the endless bombardments of artillery. This was going to be a hell of a sight when all was said and done, and I was sorry for the poor bastards who had to clean it up. But we were all thankful to have a place to rest. Many of the guys joked that dying in a church was a ticket to heaven. I don't know if that was true but I think we all secretly hoped that we would die in a place like that. It was the only place of comfort among the destruction that lingered outside its walls. The chatter didn't last long, though, since everyone wanted to take advantage of this time to rest; but I couldn't sleep. I didn't take pleasure in these moments of quiet because they made me think of Luke. Part of me just wanted to keep moving, even though my body had long ago given up on that desire. The guards tried to stay awake in shifts, though most of them fell asleep along with the rest of us. I sat awake for hours between bouts of restless slumber. I dreamt about Luke and the guys on my plane who died in the crash and I would always wake just before I was about to die. In the dream I was piloting a B-25, my brother's plane on Doolittle's mission, which was strange because I had never piloted a plane or even flown in a B-25 Mitchell. All of a sudden, parts of the plane exploded from the flack we were taking over Tokyo. Time stood still as we were floating in the air. I was begging Luke to bail out with me but he just stared ahead as if his body were frozen where it stood. Next to him were guys from my crew who I am certain went down with the Missy May. They stared at me in fear the way they had done before I bailed in Berlin. As the plane rushed closer to the ground I tried pulling them toward the door but it was dead weight. Just before the plane struck land, everything went black.

While I would like to think that this was

Luke's way of infiltrating my dreams, I suspected that the vivid insanity I was experiencing was the result of chronic dehydration. My brother was dead and after seeing the things I had seen, it was hard to have faith in anything anymore—let alone his spirit.

I woke up suddenly in the church and checked to make sure I was still alive. The way I was breathing you would think I had just run a mile. I was covered in sweat and unfamiliar with my surroundings. As I awoke I once again admired the building's architecture; it was beautiful and calming. The interior of the church wasn't as damaged as the outside. The room was illuminated by candlelight and it was like nothing I had ever seen. I doubt it would have been as nice during the day, but for that moment it offered serenity.

I didn't feel like sitting any more so I got up to check on Bill. Most of the men were scattered around the floor in a deep, peaceful sleep. They had all dropped where they stood, not wasting any time to find a pew that may have been more comfortable. Most of them huddled together under thin blankets or anything else they could find to keep warm. Every man looked the same, beaten and worn-out. I looked for Bill amongst the room of broken and torn flesh, finally locating him on the floor in a cold corner of the church. I wished I hadn't. I had never prayed so hard that a man would die; he was not the Bill I knew. Though we had all been stricken with dysentery and dehydration, Bill seemed to be having it much worse than the rest of us. In addition to his ailments, his body had become a haven for lice and other regional insects that none of us could identify. He had fallen asleep in his own excretion as the bloody, puss-filled abscesses on his face and chest grew worse from the lack of sanitation. It had been weeks since we last showered. The grime that had caked on his body layer after layer turned the color of his skin a dark gray. I couldn't believe that he had once been so strong and full of life. Though he was only twenty-two, he looked much older as if he had aged ten years since being captured. For this reason, I had no desire to see myself in the mirror; I avoided my reflection at all costs. If Bill looked that horrendous I could only imagine what I looked like. I was certain that I was just as tattered and filthy but I made a deal with myself that should I die as a result of this march I wanted to die with dignity. I saw in Bill what I didn't want for myself, and I hoped that caring for him the way that I had, would spare me the same fate. I wanted to go down fighting, but I wasn't going to do anything to instigate my own demise. I definitely wasn't the same kid who just a year ago dared the German army to kill him at the farm-house. In all honesty, I just didn't care anymore. I simply wanted the pain to end. Even the Germans were getting tired. We all just wanted to go home. It is difficult to fathom what young men will do for their country and to what lengths they will suffer to protect its secrets and defend its honor. At this point, I was simply living to survive and to ensure the safety of my buddies. I figured that since I had made it this far, giving up now would have been a waste. I also couldn't bear the thought of my mother losing another son.

As I squatted down and scraped the lice off Bill's face and neck, I watched him for a few seconds to make sure he was still breathing. I wasn't sure what they did with prisoners who couldn't continue the march. No one knew. You would hear about guys being taken into the woods and never seen again. I remember hearing about a guy who was stricken with a bad case of trench foot making it impossible for him to walk. The minute he started to become a pain in the ass—complaining and stopping for long periods of time—the Goons grabbed him while he kicked and screamed, and hauled him into the forest. Next thing the others knew, two shots were fired and they never saw or heard from him again. Now, his death was never confirmed or denied, and it could all have been more bullshit fear tactics, but I have to believe that the Germans just wanted to rid the march of dead wood so as not to prolong the experience. Most guys dropped like flies from the natural wear and tear on their bodies. I think burial just depended on the Krauts in charge. I heard of some German officers instructing airmen to move bodies off the path sometimes into wooded areas nearby, but for the most part, death littered the trail. The Goons or an Allied airman would take a dog tag off to confirm the death and notify the Army as dictated by Geneva. The Germans were usually sticklers about that shit. But no one wanted to become a casualty of the trail. It was the unknown that motivated us to stay strong.

Remnants of the envoys ahead of us served as grave reminders of the dangers we faced. Both animal and human remains were left where they fell, like road kill on a country thoroughfare for the rest of us to maneuver around. Sometimes the darkness of night was the only relief from the gruesome sights that the daylight illuminated.

Without realizing it, men would march over the remains of dead airmen whose bodies had not yet been pushed aside. The smell of rotting flesh, combined with the texture of bloody limbs that stuck to our boots in the snow, was enough to make even the toughest man sick. At least during the night we didn't have to face this reality.

We were joined on the trail by German refugees from small villages around Berlin. Like us, they carried their belongings in carts or on their backs like donkeys, hoping to escape the Russian advance. In a sick way it was comforting to know that we weren't the only ones suffering. But it killed me to watch young children enduring this march and it was no surprise that many died before reaching their destination. Some who were incredibly sick with pneumonia and hypothermia would depart the journey early as their parents detoured into the closest town braving the consequences of their decision to stay back. We would never know for sure what happened to them but I am certain that if no doctor was available their chances of survival were slim.

The reality of their situation wasn't far from our own. Each day I worried that one of my more sickly buddies would meet the same fate. They were all I had left. The only ones that could truly understand what it meant to suffer and endure pain. They were the only brothers I had and I was doing all I could to ensure their survival. It was a promise that I had made to each of them long before the march began and it was one that I intended to keep. We all helped each other since doing so was our only chance of staying alive until we somehow found a way out. As men collapsed from exhaustion, the man next to him would carry his weight until he grew too weak to continue; at that point, another man would take over. Men switched places multiple times until the one they were helping was able to walk on his own again, or until they reached a place to rest for the night. It was Hell.

Though none of us had studied the Geneva

Conventions we were pretty sure the Germans stopped playing by the rules as soon as they took us on this death march. They were running scared, fleeing the Russians, and frankly there wasn't time for their mind games. We all knew that this would soon be over and that if we could last a while longer, liberation would come. But for now we were just hoping to stay alive. I took one of Bill's dog tags and put it into my pocket. There was no way that I would rely on the Germans to do the right thing if he collapsed on the march and I vowed to personally inform his family the same as I would do with Sam's. I still had Sam's dog tag on my chain. I had kept it in my pocket for the longest time until I knew it was safe to put it around my neck. The Germans didn't seem to notice that I was wearing three tags, but to be safe, I tucked them into my shirt when they came around. I was betting that Bill would be too weak to notice or care that I had taken his tag, but if he asked I would tell him to take mine as well just as a precaution, so that he wouldn't feel like he was on his way out and realize how bad off he was.

Knowing that Bill was all right, I started back toward the wall I had been sitting against, but before I left I stared down the darkened hallway ahead. I saw Anderson and Hughes sitting against a pew and figured we could shoot the shit when they woke up so I headed that way instead. When I entered the room I noticed a Kraut guard sitting at a table by himself drinking hooch. He had been the meanest son of a bitch to all of us since our capture, delivering more pain than any other Goon at the camp, but now he seemed as beaten as the rest of us. We called him Popeye because one of his eyes noticeably bulged out of his head, and as our stint in prison had progressed, he covered it with a dark patch to appear even more terrifying once he realized that he had been bestowed with such a nickname. He was one of the ugliest sons of bitches I'd ever seen. I didn't think he noticed me walk in so I quietly headed toward the guys, figuring I would try to get some rest before the next day's hike. I knew that these opportunities to sleep wouldn't come around that often and was mad at myself for not taking advantage of it. I cursed the nightmares that kept me awake.

But before I took another step, Popeye muttered, "You're not sleeping."

I looked to see him still staring at the wall and began to answer the looming question of why I wasn't obeying my order to rest. I still couldn't believe that this man, who did not have the most inviting personality, had decided to be nice and to let us rest and have salvation from the frigid elements outside. He looked disturbed about something. As I walked toward him I said, "I wasn't tired."

He finally turned his head to acknowledge my presence. He smirked and laughed a bit under his breath. "Really! You and Eisenhower. I guess we should be watching you, too. You Americans won't rest until we're obliterated."

"No, me and Ike wouldn't get along very well

'cause I'd tell him what I really think. He's at a desk while I'm in this shithole. Maybe he'd take my place if I asked...."

"Sit down, kid. Have some hooch." He poured himself another glass and then handed me the bottle to drink what was left.

I could hardly stomach its contents. "God damn what the hell is this shit?"

"Church wine," he laughed. "It doesn't have to be good, just has to get the job done."

Even though it tasted like shit I was happy to have alcohol. "I prefer a good Tennessee whiskey but this'll do."

"Why are you Americans so arrogant? Only liking your own?"

"Why are you Germans such a pain in the ass?" To my surprise he sort of chuckled at the exchange. We both took another swig from our drinks and stared at each other waiting for one to make the next move. Then all of a sudden he resumed his thousand-mile stare and looked down at his glass then back up at me. I noticed that his eyes were wet with tears yet he didn't appear to have been crying.

"Smoke?"

"No thanks."

"You lost your brother in Tokyo, right? Do you miss him?"

At that moment I decided that I had had enough of the mind games and calmly but matter-of-factly responded to his questions. What kind of person would ask if you miss your dead brother? "With all due respect, it's not something I like to discuss and if this is another attempt at interrogation, I'm not in the mood." Looking back, I realize that he could have made my life hell for saying such a thing but I have no regrets. I was tired of them using Luke's death as leverage.

"That's not why I'm asking. It's the reason you can't sleep, isn't it Lieutenant?" he knowingly prodded.

I still couldn't trust that his motives were sincere. By now I had a history with the Krauts and we weren't exactly on good terms. I had come to the conclusion that nothing they did was out of pure kindness and that there was always a motive to their apparent concern. I stared at him and took another sip of the church wine. I was beyond flattery and I think he knew that he wasn't going to get any information from me.

But something was different this time. He needed something from me. In fact, it seemed like he was turning to me for help. Without looking into my eyes or giving in to his desire to cry, he expressed his grief. "Do you know why I brought you and your friends here, Lieutenant?"

"Because you got cold and wanted to stop."

"No," he shook his head. "It's because today I realized how wrong we've been. The last time I saw my wife and children was in the spring, just before I arrived at Stalag. My wife didn't want me to go and to be honest I didn't want to leave either. But I had no choice. I had just returned from fighting the Russians and since I no longer had sight in my right eye and was nearly crippled,

I was deemed unfit for the front lines."

I listened with care to every word though I was surprised at his honesty. Any suspicions that I had were instantly stifled and his act of kindness and care for the men began to make sense. It was so out of character for him to do such a thing and his grief at least at this moment seemed sincere. I saw the pain in his eyes as he fought back tears. It was a lot for me to take and my exhaustion was beginning to catch up with me, so I kept drinking the bad hooch to stay awake because I wanted to be alert for the rest of this conversation.

"I was assigned to Luft III to finish my commitment to the Reich. My children cried as my mother and wife tried to calm them. I hated to leave and something told me that I would never see them again ... little did I know that they would be the ones to die instead of me." He paused and stared in the same way I had the day I learned that Luke had died. Just like me, he wasn't there when his family was killed and he was left with the guilt of not being able to protect them. He was forced to find out from someone he barely knew that he would now face this world alone. I had been so fearful of seeing my own reflection all this time but fate intervened and forced me to look. His thousand-mile stare may as well have been my face and his dirt-covered body and callused skin could have sufficed as my own. I took another swig of wine and sat back in my chair, staring at the wall. At that moment I would have stared at anything but his face—it was too much to bear.

"I always thought I would be the one to die in this war. Not my family ... after all, I deserve it. The things I've done ... the things I've seen. Terrible things. If God were gracious he would allow me to trade places with my family. I gladly would have," he said with an intensity that was driven by love instead of hate.

With that outburst, tears came running down the sides of his cheeks. This tough man who had been involved in such violent acts was actually human. He must have felt like I would understand because he didn't apologize for his behavior or attempt to save face by exerting his power as a Kraut. It was actually the most civilized and honest moment I'd experienced with anyone since I had been captured. We were just two guys talking like buddies. I never thought a moment like that would happen with a German, especially on a death march to Munich.

He collected himself enough to speak again. "I'm very sorry for what we've put you through. The things we have done and the information we've used to get what we want. For what? They think they have really succeeded when they watch you cry about your family ... but where does it get them? You people don't talk." He reached into his coat pocket and took out a picture of his wife and kids in front of an old house. He held it in his hand and stared at it for a while before handing it to me. "The one on the left is Angelika, she was my youngest. She had the greenest eyes you ever saw. Ben was my boy

... he loved to run around our garden. He would play until it got too dark to see and his mother would call him in for the night. His mother ...." He could barely speak as he thought of his wife, "His mother, Talia, was everything. I don't know how she did it, how could I leave her for this. I should have stayed right there with her. I shouldn't have left her. Ever. This god-damn war."

I sat there listening in horror. This man had truly lost everything. If he managed to survive this war he would return to an empty home. I felt sorrow for his pain and wished that I could help him, but nothing I could do or say would ease that kind of hurt.

I knew that if any of the men woke to find me drinking with Popeye, they would probably think I was "turned" or something. Or they would just wonder what the hell was going on, but I figured that I had a good enough reputation with the men for any suspicions to be quelled. I had been to Hell and back for most of these guys, suffering for them on many occasions, a conversation with a Kraut couldn't possibly deplete all of that hard-earned trust.

I listened carefully as Popeye continued our conversation. "I remember your first day ... you were smarter than the others—you never tried to escape. Some people think it's their duty to escape but it only complicates things. You might as well shoot yourself—it's the weak who try to run because they think that they aren't meant to be held captive. But the very fact that they allowed themselves to become a prisoner is ... how is it that you stay this strong?"

I had no answer for this question. Strong was not a word I would have used to describe myself, especially considering the way I broke down after hearing of my brother's death. I sat in silence for a few minutes until Popeye finally said, "Get some rest, Lieutenant. You're going to need it."

I stood up from the table, leaving the wine for him to finish. "Sorry about your wife and kids ... that's rough. They didn't deserve what happened to them." I left that room feeling guilty for all the air raids I had been involved in executing. I was certain that we had killed more innocent civilians than we did enemy soldiers while dropping the bombs wherever we wanted to, believing that any collateral damage was an acceptable casualty of war if it meant annihilating the enemy in the process. As careful as we tried to be, accidents happened; but we were always able to fly over the consequences of our actions without having to confront or bear witness to the destruction below. Seeing the picture of his family killed me. I would never forget their faces for the rest of my life. It was awful to think that they were helpless and terrified, killed in a routine explosion that no one in the air even cared about having hit. This fucking war.

After that night Popeye was different—his once torturous demeanor gave way to sympathy and, like all of us, the desire to see an end to the fighting. His subordinates began to question his authority and his loyalty to the Nazis, but when

Popeye became aware of their concerns, he beat one of his own men half to death. I think he was disgusted by the men he served with and like many of his older comrades, had started to believe less of Hitler's insanity. Needless to say, it was a refreshing sight to see torture inflicted on someone from the other side for a change. After that, no one messed with Popeye, but morale among the Germans quickly deteriorated and we all became prisoners of the same war suffering together with each mile of the march.

A few weeks went by before we finally settled in a permanent camp outside of Munich. Conditions were just a notch above squalor and men were at death's door, though at least we were in the shelter of barracks again. The march had taken its toll on our already weakened bodies and left us too fatigued to feel the pains of hunger. Little did we know that our fate was about to change drastically. On the morning of April 29th the Russians finally broke through. Woken by a hail of bullets and the sound of ammunition pounding the camp, I grabbed Bill and pulled him under the bunk, staying as low as I could as bullets stormed through windows and blasted walls. Bill remained unresponsive though he opened his eyes for a moment to witness the ordeal, likely wishing that this would be the end of our misery and that we'd all be killed instantly.

All at once, the firing ceased and was immediately replaced by shouts from Russian officers spouting demands at every Goon on duty. Me and some of the other fellas crawled slowly toward the window. As we peeked through, we saw Russian guards pushing Kraut officers to the ground and kicking their heads just as the Germans had done to each one of us when we were captured. While witnessing such atrocities, each man strong enough to realize what was happening smirked with vengeance in enjoyment of the sight. It took everything in us not to join in, but no one knew what the Russians would do with us. One by one the men exited the room, taking their first steps toward freedom, raising their arms in surrender, making it clear that we were Americans by pointing at the flag patch on our uniform. Many roamed the compound in search of friendly faces and guidance from the liberators regarding our release. However, the language barrier and overall confusion about protocol left the former prisoners more frustrated than before. There is nothing worse than being saved but unable to leave. So there we sat, waiting again.

As men gathered within guarded gates, the most beautiful sound of rumbling tanks moved through the camp and brought tears to our eyes. In true American fashion, the US liberators latched onto the barbed wire fence that had been the instrument of our confinement, and in one motion tore it down and rolled into the camp like bulldozers. Some men cheered while others cried, or remained silent with relief. After nearly a year of captivity and months on the road, we would all be going home. We had survived the worst the Krauts could throw at us and as a reward we would be returning to the peace and joy of family. As I stood in silence, the only thing on my mind was Luke. I feared this day because the true horror for me was at home where I would be haunted by painful memories and an empty bed in the room next to mine.

Men too weak to celebrate retired to their barracks to be alone as they clung to the hands of medics faced with the daunting task of treating their wounds. Others cried, hugging their liberators—most of them kids our age who could have easily been prisoners themselves. I watched as American officers rounded up the Krauts like cattle and pushed them to the ground securing their position with a boot to the back of the neck. Out of respect, the Russians allowed our guys to take over. They proceeded to hand guns and bayonets to airmen to kill a Goon of their choice—needless to say the most hot-tempered guards were some of the first to go. As blood seeped from the lifeless bodies, I was astonished that these young men, after having experienced such painful captivity, could then allow these guards to get off so easily. None of us had been spared the agony of mental and physical anguish that the guards surely would have experienced had they not been killed. As good as it must have felt to rid the world of another asshole and to get the revenge the liberated prisoners deserved, it wasn't for me. Some men were driving bullets into the same dead man just to seek closure, but with each bullet, I grew more disgusted.

On my way back to my barracks, a familiar voice called out, "Hey, Jake! Hey buddy." I turned to find Prescott from North Compound holding a Kraut sidearm. Looking at the guard with disgust, Prescott said matter-of-factly, "Hey we saved one for ya ... you know, one of those sons of bitches that messed with you about Luke."

His mention of Luke got my attention. He pointed toward the man ... it was Popeye. Not knowing about our conversation at the church, the other men probably thought I would enjoy killing him. I knew what he was going through and almost wondered if I should be the one to end his life before someone else did. With the gun in my hand, I saw him give me a look begging for me to pull the trigger. The men gathered around me, cheering in anticipation and shouting, "This one's for Luke! Do it for your brother!" But I couldn't bear the thought of taking yet another life, especially Popeye's, in Luke's name. I decided right there that I wouldn't kill another soul and that if any more Krauts died in this war it wouldn't be at my hand. I saw the look of both disappointment and relief in Popeye's eyes as tears filled mine. I retracted my arm and gave the weapon back to Prescott, who patted me on the shoulder.

"I can't ...."

"It's okay, buddy ...."

While the guys were disappointed, the gun eventually changed hands and Popeye's fate was sealed. With tears in my eyes I walked back toward the barracks, not wanting to turn around and witness the sight. Within seconds a single shot was fired as a group of men stood over Popeye cheering like the animals they had become. I cried for my friend and returned to my temporary confinement, waiting for the excitement to die down in the quad.

As it turns out, our orders didn't come for a few weeks but when they did, most of the men took it upon themselves to depart quietly and leave behind the pain of prison life as well as the friends they had made during their stay. After a week of being rehabilitated, I left for Paris and enjoyed my new-found sense of reality. The city was buzzing. To look at Paris, one wouldn't believe that a war had just been fought. It was as if nothing had happened; as if our suffering was old news. Suddenly the careless nightlife I had found superior to home seemed far removed from the comforts of Nebraska. Women I had never met kissed and hugged me in celebration once they saw my uniform. They could be happy because their war was over. Once their buildings and houses were rebuilt all that would be left of these hellish years were bitter memories soon to be forgotten as other distractions came along.

But for me, a new war was just about to begin. I saw no value in a life without Luke and found myself wishing that I had died when given the chance. I hadn't seen Bill since he was taken to the hospital after our liberation. He was in pretty bad shape and I feared that he wouldn't survive much longer. I couldn't leave for the States until I knew he was all right. When I arrived in England, I headed straight to the hospital and found his bed. As I walked through the door of the ward filled with broken men, I reached into my pocket to grab Bill's dog tag and found it stuck to Sam's, whose tag I finally took off my chain after my release. I passed bed after bed, wondering how in the hell I wasn't as bad off as the rest of these guys. Men screamed for help begging me to put an end to their misery. I stopped at the bed of a soldier whose amputated leg was bleeding profusely. As if that weren't bad enough, a wound in his stomach was oozing blood and fluids into my hands as I held him together just before a doctor rushed over to treat him. It took everything in me not to be sick at the sight. The awful thing was that I could see Sam's eyes and the features of the Kraut I killed in the forest in this poor kid's face. Not wanting to greet Bill with bloody hands, I asked the nurse where I could wash up and she pointed me toward a large bucket of water sitting in the middle of the room. I dipped both of my hands in the bucket and dried them on the same handkerchief I had relied on in the forest. Though it was still covered in Bill's dried blood and sweat, it did the trick and dried my hands just enough to be effective. Just past the water was Bill's bed. He was sound asleep amid all the chaos. I stood over him for a bit wondering if I should wake him or let him rest. I decided that he probably wouldn't be in the mood for visitors so I left his dog tag on his chest and patted his arm. As I walked away a familiar voice spoke. "Hey shithead

... you come here just to leave?"

I turned around smiling. "Figured you were dead to the world, didn't want to bother you. Nice to see you haven't changed any," I said.

"Grab a chair, Jake ... what's with your hand? That blood?"

"Nothin, just cut it on a beer bottle. Crazy night in Paris." I wasn't about to tell him that I just had my hand in the stomach of a guy two beds next to him.

"Sorry I missed that. I been a little .... "

"I know," I said. "Just happy you made it."

He pulled his dog tag off the sheet and stared at the metal, running his thumb over his name and serial number. He held it up and looked at me. "Bet you thought you were gonna have to send this one home to my mom didn't you?" he asked.

"Never crossed my mind," I replied.

He looked at me in disbelief then looked down at the dog tag, tossing it back onto the bed. "Got a letter from Faith ... guess she married

Danny while we were in prison. Sorry, Jake," he said.

"Yeah ... I figured she would. We weren't meant to be."

"Maybe it's for the best, you know?" he said.

"How so?" I asked.

"Guys like us ... seeing what we've seen. How in the hell could she understand? She already lost Tommy. She don't need that trouble." he said. "Danny never saw the shit we saw. He won't wake up in the middle of the night crazy as hell thinking he's back in Berlin. Don't tell me you don't think about it, Jake," he prodded.

I didn't respond. I just stared at him and looked away.

"Well maybe it's just me then ...." he said after a while.

I was hesitant to share my thoughts, but eventually said, "It's not just you, Bill. The other day I was at this bread stand in Paris chatting with the owner. Everything was okay for a while until he finally gave me the loaf I paid for. Then I realized that I was about to eat prison food. I got hold of the loaf and started bawling my eyes out. Then I dropped it where I stood, feeling as helpless as I did in the goddamn camp. I screamed 'SHOOT ME! SHOOT ME!' Passersby had no idea what the hell was wrong. Even the cops avoided me."

"I know Jake: bread, water, and soup. I'm always thinking about it, can't look at the shit no more, makes me sick every time," he said.

"I can't explain it, but it reminds me of Popeye," I responded.

"Jake, I can't sleep at night. I wake up screaming and beating the walls and anything else in the way, thinking about Stalag, I guess," he said. "One time I grabbed Dr. Drimman, shoving him to the wall and screaming at him in Kraut. How in the hell can I speak Kraut in my sleep? I don't know how to speak Kraut."

"You'll be fine Bill, just give it time."

"Jake! Time's just making it worse ... time isn't bringing Tommy back. It's not gonna bring

Luke back. They're dead. We're dead," he said. I sat in silence. "You still got Sam's stuff? We gotta tell his mom. She deserves to know what really happened," he continued.

"Yeah, got it ... but don't worry about it, I'll send her a letter for the both of us. No reason you should have to deal with that right now," I told him.

"Just make sure you say we were both there and that it was my fault. I froze up. I let him down," he said.

Annoyed that he still blamed himself for what happened in the forest, I said, "Stop talking like that. No one could have saved him. He was shot up so bad. Don't put that on yourself. What we did out there ... me killing that Kraut, it had to be done,"

"You were always the strong one Jake. I'm gonna miss you," he said.

"You take care of yourself Bill ... we'll hook back up in the States," I assured him.

"Sorry about your brother," he responded as

I got out of my chair.

"Yeah... yeah, you too, Bill,"

"I just hope it was worth it," he said.

"Yeah ... me, too." I shook his hand and walked away. We were the closest thing to brothers each of us had left. The only ones who had been there to witness each other suffering and could understand each other's pain. We'd been to Hell and back together but our separation was inevitable; sadly, we would part for good that day, never to see each other again.

I left the hospital and found I was just in time to catch the next boat to the States. The seas were rough and I gave way to sickness ... being stuck in those close quarters, I couldn't wait to hit land. I was sick of being away and had become claustrophobic from prison. My mind was never far from home. Every day, I thought about Luke and about seeing my poor mother's face again. I wondered if she knew, or if I would have to break the news to her that Luke had been killed. Several times I thought of contacting his buddies from the Lucky Lady who had survived the crash, but part of me didn't want to hear any more about it. I sat with the same thousand-mile stare I had developed at Stalag. Occasionally men would try to strike up a conversation or sell me some of their souvenirs from their various campaigns, but I was in no mood to talk and wasn't interested in buying—I just wanted to get home.

From the ship I boarded a train in New York City—another city I had no interest in seeing. I spent a few months at a base in San Antonio where I was properly treated for the wound on my shoulder and finally discharged from the Air Force. It had been a long three years. I definitely wasn't the same kid as before, and going home scared me more than anything I had endured overseas. I didn't know how to go home; the guilt of knowing that I would be at my mother's front door, instead of Luke, was enough to drive me crazy. This made the train ride to Nebraska almost unbearable. At each stop I grew nervous as we inched closer and closer, approaching Lincoln. I wrote letters to Bill and to Charlie Shaw in celebration of our survival and concern for their whereabouts. Looking outside at the landscape, I saw with new perspective the nature that Luke had so appreciated during our last visit. The train traveled on and as night fell I tried to sleep, but as I closed my eyes I saw Popeye's face. He was angry that I refused to take his life at the camp. Then I realized that since Popeye and I had bonded, death at the hands of someone who understood would have been more honorable than death delivered by someone as a means of revenge. I had let yet another down. The distinct sounds of Mission 13 then filled my continuing nightmare. Flashes, ammo piercing through the skin of the Missy May, the screams and sheer panic in the voices of the crew and a collage of terrifying memories of captivity overwhelmed my slumber. I awoke, screaming, to the voice of a porter.

"Wake up son, you havin' a bad dream."

"I don't know what's wrong. I keep … I keep seeing things … I keep hearing things … I can't put it out of my mind. Who are you?" I asked.

The old man replied, "I'm Sammy, the porter on this here train. You?"

"Jake, Jake Thompson."

"You look like shit, Jake," the old man said. A cold look came over his face as he stared into my eyes. "Son, you shell-shocked."

"What do you mean?" I asked, to which he answered, "You know. Who got killed? Brother? Buddy?"

"Both," I replied.

"Have a drink, Son." A drink was the last thing I needed but he poured two glasses—one for me and one for him. He grabbed the seat across from me. "The trenches was dark and cold … disease running rampant through the camp. Hadn't seen the enemy in days. I was playing cards with my buddies 'til it got too dark to see.

All of a sudden bullets start flying from across the field. Cannon fire blasting us … I sat up with my gun, ducking low enough not to get hit but holding my gun just high enough to shoot. Johnson was right next to me the whole time, head down same as me. We was shooting at nothing … couldn't even see. Next thing I know some guy down the trenches shouts, 'Johnson get your ass over here!' Johnson stands up and looks back at me to make sure I'm all right, as bullet after bullet pounds his chest. He fell right on top of me … there was nothing I could do. As soon as I heard 'cease fire,' I pulled him toward me and checked if he was still alive. He died quick … I sat there staring at him for the rest of the night. We was best friends since school. Rode bikes together, played stickball, died together. Never was the same after that night." He drank the rest of his whiskey and stared off into the distance lost in his own thoughts. I drank the rest of my whiskey, thinking about Luke. "It does something to you. Changes who you are, how you see things. When you see a man die, knowing that he had so much to live for. But best thing you can do is move on, Son. The good Lord spared you in this one so you owe it to Him to find out why."

When I awoke, the sun was shining and the train was moving fast toward home. Two empty glasses were sitting on the table in front of me. It was a quarter past ten and after a rough night of sleep, I needed to stretch my legs and figured I would run into Sammy so we could finish our conversation. I grabbed my glass hoping to find an open bar ready and willing to fill her up but it was too early for that, the bar was closed. A man was cleaning the top of the wooden slab when I walked up to him. "Would I be wrong in pointing out that it's five o'clock in Berlin about now and where I come from that's happy hour?" I asked him.

"Sorry, son ... bottles are put away, we don't bring 'em out 'til six."

"Would you make an exception? I'd be happy

to make it worth your while." I pulled twenty dollars of my poker winnings out of my pocket.

"Put that away." He pulled a flask from his jacket pocket and filled my glass. He looked around and said, "Anyone asks you didn't get that from me."

"Your secret's safe ... I'm not talking."

"You all right, kid? Have a rough night?"

"Guess you could say that ...." I never looked him in the eyes but I could feel him staring at me.

"Air Force?" he asked.

"Yeah...."

"My brother was in the Air Force," he informed me.

"Oh yeah? He dead like mine?" He didn't know how to respond and I wasn't in the mood to say any more about it, so he grew silent. "Hey, you know where I can find Sammy?"

"Who?"

"Sammy ... he's a porter on this train, talked to him last night."

"No Sammy I know ... you sure he wasn't a passenger?"

"I'm sure ... he was wearing a porter's uniform and everything. Tall, dark, dark hair."

"Might wanna ease up on the booze, kid ... just a thought."

He walked away, believing that I was crazy. What the hell, was my mind playing tricks on me? No, he was there but why didn't anyone know him? I spent the rest of the trip wondering if I really was losing my mind and terrified that this was only the beginning of what life after the war would be.

LINCOLN, NEBRASKA
December 1945

As I approached the front steps I hesitated, terrified of disappointing my mother. The house was decorated in celebration of the holidays. Handmade paper angels hung in the window and I could see the tree through the empty space in the glass. In the window also hung a banner with two stars—one blue and one gold. They knew about Luke. I never wished so hard that I could trade places with my brother. It took everything in me not to run toward the old oak tree that Luke and I occupied as kids and never return. That was the only place I was drawn to, that felt comfortable anymore. But I knew that it wouldn't be right. My parents deserved to know I was home, though I knew I wasn't the son who should've returned. I knocked twice on the front door and anxiously waited for someone to answer. I could hear my sisters laughing and the humming of Christmas carols through the door. I felt like I was about to impose on a happy occasion and immediately regretted coming home today of all days. As footsteps approached I braced for whoever was coming. Seconds later my mother appeared, looking both shocked and relieved at my presence. Before I could say anything, she threw her arms around me and cried tears of joy and relief. She eventually broke her embrace and grabbed both of my hands staring at me with pride. I couldn't stand to look at her anymore; I was overwhelmed with guilt. "Look, Mom ... about Luke...."

"I know," she said reassuringly. "We heard the news a few months back and we're dealing with it best we can, Son."

"I'm sorry ... it should've been me, Mom."

To my surprise, this comment upset her. With an icy glare she stared into my eyes, penetrating my soul with her gaze. "Don't you ever say that, you hear? It is not up to you. That was his cross to bear, not yours." As tears poured down our cheeks, I had never felt my mother's love more than I did that day. "I'm proud of you baby ... you did us proud. Me, your father, your sisters, John ... all of us. When we heard you was a POW we didn't know ...."

"Mom ... it's okay," I assured her. Still not letting go of my hand, she led me to the familiar living room where my sisters played with dolls and my father sat reading the paper. "Joe, look who's here! It's Jake ... he's back!"

My father slowly lowered his newspaper and approached me with the same look of disbelief. He walked casually toward the two of us and extended his hand. "Welcome home, Son. Merry Christmas."

"Thanks, Pop." Since he wasn't an emotional

man it was unlikely that I would see any tears fall from his eyes. But I think my mother cried enough tears for the both of them. That night we enjoyed a family dinner like no other, though my father finally fell apart when he glanced at the chair that Luke used to occupy ....

"We don't even know where he is, bastards killed him and we never got him back. Bad enough he's gone but we don't even have a place to go visit." What do you say to a man whose son has been killed in action, especially a man like my father who wanted nothing more than to trade places with his son? He left the room and went to bed, stopping only to look at the Christmas tree he had chopped down himself— something that us boys had always done since I can remember. This year he had done it alone, just as he had for all the years of the war.

"He's just got to adjust is all ...." my mother insisted. There was nothing I could say in response.

Later, I went upstairs to tell my sisters good-night and had to stave off requests for war adventure stories in place of their usual bedtime fairytales. Happy that they were safe, I waited until after they fell asleep to leave the room and head outside. I couldn't bring myself to go into my bedroom, because everything in there reminded me of my brother.

As the snow fell that Christmas Eve, I could only think of Luke and the memories from the last holiday I spent in prison. In the silence I heard my buddies singing somber Christmas carols in the darkness of night, confined to their respective cells. A rhythm of sobs and cries of agony were all that kept an otherwise non-existent beat. I could hear Skip Jones revealing the painful truth about Luke's crash, ending what had been months of speculation and lies from my initial interrogation. It is these memories that my father would never understand. No one would understand. As I watched flakes fall from the sky, I thought of everything that had happened and was reminded of the fact that Luke wouldn't be coming home—all of his dreams were gone. I wasn't sure how I would face these painful memories and relive our horrors each day. I cried alone in the stables next to the oak tree where Luke and I had spent our time; where we made a break for California and where I promised to enter the Air Corps upon graduation. I cried at the loss of my brother.

As I went to lie in a bed of hay in the old stables, I drifted off to a time long ago, thinking of better days when Luke and I were young and carefree.

"Jake, it's me, Luke."

"It can't be—you died in the Pacific."

"Yeah, I know. Are you gonna leave me here? I wanna come home."

"Luke, where are you? They never said."

"We were running out of fuel off the coast of China. Our pilot came over the cabin speaker. 'We're going down and it's gonna be a hard water landing. Get somewhere safe and brace your-selves. Once we hit the water get the hell out of this death trap.' Jake I was scared, cuz I didn't know how to swim."

"We came in hard and the plane broke apart. Me and Moore were in the belly of the 'Lady' and then everything went black. When I came to, I tried Brother, I tried to swim but I just couldn't. My arms and legs were broken. Moore was killed instantly. I had to push him off me so I could try to get out of the plane. Bradley was yelling at me to hold on as he tried to get to me but the current was rough. I gave up, Jake, I died a quitter. All those years of tellin' you never to quit, never to give up, and I died a quitter."

"Bradley and a couple of the fellas dragged my body to shore and buried me before the Japs captured them. If they had just left me they might have gotten away. I'm on the beach, read the letter from Bradley and he'll tell you where. Bring me home ...."

I awoke terrified. The letter my mother had given to me from Luke's navigator, Chase Bradley (the Lucky Lady's only surviving crew member after the rest died in Jap prison), was in my coat pocket, but I just hadn't been able to bring myself to read it. I didn't want to read about my brother's death from a man who would confirm all my worst fears. But the fact that Bradley had been through Hell as a POW and still wrote to me about Luke made me think that reading it was the least I could do. I slowly broke the seal on the envelope and pulled the letter from inside. It was perfectly creased and folded, marking squares on the paper. His cursive was neat as a pin, every word endorsing the fact that my brother had died a tragic death on the banks of the China Sea—just as Skip Jones had confirmed months before.

November 1945

Lt. Thompson:

I hope this letter finds you well and that you are safe at home where you belong this holiday season. This war has proven to be more hellish than anyone could have imagined, claiming the lives of honorable men, young and healthy, who should never have been in such a position. I can only speak for what I have endured as a prisoner of the Japs and can tell you with certainty that the Devil was present in those camps as I am sure he was in Germany. However, I am the lucky one. By now you must know that your brother Luke was killed during the Tokyo operation. As his co-crewman, I feel in my heart each day that I was a coward for choosing life when he and Moore had already given theirs. To you and your family I would like to extend my deepest apologies for failing to bring Luke home alive. Though I did everything I could to ensure our survival, my talents as a navigator proved inferior to the circumstances. Luke fought to survive but his injuries were so extensive that death was inevitable. Though it may not seem like it, he was spared from the torture that lay before him had he lived. I gladly would have taken my own life in prison had it not been for those men and a need to get this message to your family. By the time I reached Luke, he was floating lifeless in the water. I pulled him to shore with the help of the pilot and co-pilot and laid him on the sand. A Chinese woman came down from the hills and I grabbed Luke's weapon thinking she was a Jap. She raised her arms in surrender, assuring us that she was not going to harm our crew. In her hand was a Chinese flag, further proving that she was not our enemy. She knelt down and wiped the blood from Luke's face and neck (injuries he sustained from the crash) and prayed over his body. We watched in disbelief as she blessed and cared for him as one of her own. She pointed to a spot on the beach where a hole existed, far enough from the tide so that he would not be swept in by the current. We buried him there and covered his body with sand so that the Japs would never find him. We did the same for Moore. I took Luke's dog tag and his cross and put it on my chain (You'll find them enclosed in this envelope). We all promised that we would tell the Allies where they were buried when we were rescued. Unfortunately, Japs were coming down the hill fast and the Chinese woman ran into hiding in the reefs. We wanted her to go, figuring that if she was caught helping us she would surely be killed and no one would ever find Luke and send him home. We raised our arms in surrender and were beaten with bayonets and bamboo sticks until our legs were broken—bruised and bloody. This torture continued for the next year as man after man died in prison. If disease didn't get to you, the Japs would. Luke died quick, sparing him this experience. While I have been given the gift of life when Luke lost his, I want you to understand that your brother's death will haunt me for the rest of mine. Please tell your mother that I have arranged for his body to be recovered from the beach and that he will be coming home. I hope that she can forgive me for my shortcomings as a navigator and as a human being. For me the suffering will continue. I only hope that you can find some peace in knowing that your brother died a hero of the highest order and that his death will not be forgotten by his fellow 'Raiders', his brothers from Eglin, who failed to make the ultimate sacrifice in the name of war.

Sincerely;

Lt. Chase Bradley

I hated that Chase blamed himself for what happened to Luke and decided that I couldn't possibly hold him responsible for what was not his fault—just as none of us could carry such a burden. I tossed the letter into a pile of hay trying my best not to think about my ordeal at the farmhouse and stood on my feet. I kept walking until I approached the edge of our land spanning miles and miles across the region. Dense layers of fog strolled calmly by, blanketing the earth with their presence. Though I could barely see, I knelt down and ran my hand through the ground, picking up a handful of dirt, sifting the rocks and twigs with my fingers. As I released my grip and let it slide down the palm of my hand, I stared into the abyss, deciding at that moment that I would live the life my brother couldn't. Nebraska wasn't so bad anymore and the quiet no longer terrified me as it had before. This was my gift for surviving and my brother would never be far from my side as I lived a life for both of us. Together we would find peace.

AFTERWORD

I've lived a long life happy at times, sad most of the time, lost in my own mind and misunderstood by many. How could they know? How could they possibly comprehend what I have endured? The blood on my hands of those whose lives I have taken in combat, the memories of my time in captivity, the torturous beatings and near death experiences, and perhaps most painful of all, living an entire life without my brother.

Now years later, as they lay me to rest in this cemetery, I look down from the heavens upon my grave where I see my flag-draped coffin. I listen to the sound of Taps playing in the distance and wince with each round fired in a twenty-one gun salute.

As I watch, two young men ceremoniously remove and fold the crisp American flag and offer it to my surviving family. I look to my right and find my brother beside me. With tears running down both cheeks he apologizes for leaving me alone to face a difficult life after his death. "Welcome home, Brother. You fought bravely and survived not only on the hellish battlefield, but in life after the war—you made me proud, you always made me proud."

I am finally free of the demons that haunted me and as I look down on my grave, I finally understand the true "*Cost of Courage.*"

To my grand uncles Donald and Richard,
I thank you for your service; I will never forget your
sacrifices.
May you both rest in peace.

With all my love and respect,
Kelly

CPSIA information can be obtained
at www.ICGtesting.com
Printed in the USA
FSOW02n1344300816
24387FS